MW00425732

GIRL OF THE MANZANOS

by

Barbara Spencer Foster

First Fiction Series

SANTA FE

Sunstone books may be purchased for educational, business, or sales promotional use.
For information please write: Special Markets Department, Sunstone Press, P.O. Box 2321, Santa Fe, New Mexico 87504-2321.

FIRST EDITION

10 9 8 7 6 5 4 3 2 1

Library of Congress Cataloging-in-Publication Data:

Foster, Barbara Spencer, 1927–
Girl of the Manzanos / by Barbara Spencer Foster.– 1st ed.
p. cm.
ISBN: 0-86534-313-6 (hardcover) –ISBN: 0-86534-331-4 (paper)
1. Frontier and poineer life–Fiction. 2. Lumber trade–Fiction. 3. Manzano Mountains (N.M.)–Fiction. 4. New Mexico–Fiction. I. Title.

PS3556.O7575 G5 2001
813' .54–dc21 00-049657

Published by SUNSTONE PRESS
Post Office Box 2321
Santa Fe, NM 87504-2321 / USA
(505) 988-4418 / *orders only* (800) 243-5644
FAX (505) 988-1025
www.sunstonepress.com

This book is dedicated to my father, Roy A. Spencer, who told the stories, and to my grandfather and grandmother, Benjamin and Sarah Spencer, who lived the stories.

ACKNOWLEDGEMENTS

I wish to thank these people for their encouragement and help with this book: my son, Mike Foster, who gave me the computer and told me to "Write," my daughters-in-law, Mary and Patti Foster, my other sons, Joe and Jim Foster, my son-in-law, Greg Ames, my sisters, Patricia Ann Allen, Verna Nell Whitehead, and Helen Spivey, my brother, Richard Spencer, my brothers-in-law, Bob Allen, Roy Whitehead, and Joe Spivey, my sisters-in-law, Lula Spencer and Bonnie Spencer, and my niece, Tana Jefferson. You have all been an inspiration in my life and in my writing.

I wish to thank my dear friends, Sister Rita Barreras and Elsie Sachs for their help with Spanish usage. Muchas gracias, mis amigas!

A special thanks goes to my brother, Roy Spencer, Jr., who has been my consultant in my writing. Because of his advice, I'm sure my book is a better finished product. I appreciate your interest and help very much, dear brother.

I especially wish to thank my cousin, Frances Autry Jones, for all her support and research help. Without her, there would have been no book. Thanks, Cuz! You are my hero! I admire you and love you very much.

My greatest thanks goes to my daughter, Susan Ames, who is a loving wife and mother, and her mother's most loyal and competent helper. Her father called her a "Little Princess" the day she was born. She is that and much more.

Some of my greatest inspiration came from my grandchildren, who were interested in my writing, suggested possible plots, and read parts of the book. Thanks, especially to Jack, and all the others, Lacey, Brad, Bobby, Lance, Patrice, Jaclyn, David, Steven, Ashley, Brian, Sean, and our beautiful new little star, Nicole Spencer Ames. You are all my precious points of light.

INTRODUCTION

My grandfather, Benjamin Boyd Spencer, came to the foothills of the Manzano Mountains in 1887. He established a thriving lumber business and married the schoolteacher he brought in to teach the children of his sawmill workers. They had four sons, Roy, John, Charlie, and Floyd. I have named the family in my story after my Spencer ancestors.

I grew up listening to the stories of these hardy pioneers. My father was a great storyteller, and he made life in that era in those mountains very real to me. This book I have written is a book of fiction, but many of the events in the story are based on true stories my father told me.

I have attempted to write a book that paints an accurate picture of life in the Manzano Mountains in the early statehood period of New Mexico history. My father was born in New Mexico when it was a territory, but he actually remembered the statehood celebration that was held in his community. The account that he gave of that event inspired me to write this book.

New Mexico became a state in 1912, and that is a long time ago in our history, but I think it is important to pay homage to the brave pioneers who had the courage to join the original settlers, the Indians, in establishing homes on this frontier.

This book is a tribute to all those people, not just my grandparents, who helped build the state into the wonderful place it is today.

—Barbara Spencer Foster

1

Bright New Mexico sunlight filtered down through the pinon and pine branches of the trees sheltering the picnic meadow. The date was July 4, 1912. New Mexico was a new state in the Union, having been officially made the forty-seventh star on the flag the previous January 5th. The small community of Eastview, nestled in the foothills of the Manzano Mountains, was acknowledging this momentous occasion as it celebrated the Fourth of July.

Ben Spencer, the man who had organized the celebration, checked the food cooking on the outdoor fireplace. Nothing like the smells of the forest intermingled with the delicious aromas of chili and pinto beans to make a man's stomach jump with joy, he thought. He wiped his sweaty forehead and ran his fingers through his thick wavy auburn hair just beginning to be tinged with gray. He stepped over into the shade of a pine tree to observe the celebration scene with a smile of satisfaction.

A musical group consisting of a fiddle, a guitar, and a mandolin softly sounded out the strains of the *Over the Waves Waltz* as sunbonneted women and overalled men sat on the benches enjoying the music. Their work-worn faces were relaxed and smiling as they visited and enjoyed the festivities.

Many of the celebrants were employed at the sawmill Ben Spencer operated; the others were farmers and ranchers. They had been here since early afternoon and had either watched or taken part in the games and races Ben had organized. Now they were looking forward to a picnic dinner, a skit from the children, and dancing that would last long into the night. There was also a featured speaker, Judge Jeffrey Corbin from Socorro, who would sound the praises of New Mexico and the Union.

Sadie Spencer, Ben's wife, motioned for him to lift the heavy iron kettles full of beans and chili onto the picnic table. Setting a pot of beans carefully down on the table among the bowls of potato salad, cole slaw, pickles and relishes, homemade rolls, cakes, and fruit pies, Ben said with a grin, "The food looks wonderful, Sadie."

Sadie had brought an apronful of silverware from the house which was not far from the picnic meadow. Just as she was transferring her load to the table, a small boy suddenly dove under her skirts. Silverware flew in every direction as Sadie dropped her apron and grabbed the edge of the table for support. "Roy!" she gasped in consternation. "What in the world are you doing? You nearly knocked me over."

Ben and Sadie's youngest boy held tightly to his mother's legs as he thrust his tousled blonde head around her skirt. "Marcus was after me," he said defensively. "I won all his marbles, and he said I cheated. I didn't, Mama, I didn't. I won 'em fair and square." Roy pursed his lips and thrust out his small square chin in the direction of a boy about his size who had stopped his chase a few feet back when Roy sought the protection of his mother's skirts.

Ben quickly set down the pot of chili he was holding and grabbed for his son's arm. Roy stood stiffly under his father's tight grasp as Ben motioned for the other boy to come closer. "What's the problem, son?" he asked the boy who stood looking uncertainly from Roy to Ben Spencer.

"He used a steely for a shooter," the boy said in a rush of words. "And it ain't fair cause it knocks more marbles out of the ring than a regular shooter."

"How many marbles did you win?" Ben asked as he looked down into his young son's face.

Roy hesitated and twisted nervously under his father's straight gaze. "I don't know," he muttered. "Maybe nine or ten."

"And that's all the marbles I have," the other boy said with a break in his voice as tears started to fill his eyes.

"Give him his marbles back," Ben said to Roy. "You have plenty of marbles. You don't need his."

"But . . .," Roy started to protest.

"No buts," Ben said firmly. "And let this be a lesson to both of you. Everyone loses when you gamble, isn't that right, Sadie?" Ben cast an amused glance at his wife who returned his look with an exasperated sigh.

Roy reluctantly started pulling marbles out of his bulging pockets, and the other boy picked out the ones that were his. When all his property had been retrieved he turned with a satisfied look and started to leave. Sadie detained him with a hand on his shoulder. "Marcus, wait a minute. It's time to go and get dressed for the skit." Taking her son by the hand she continued, "Come on, Roy, you must get dressed, too."

This was too much for Roy who was still seething over the outcome of the marble dispute. The last thing he wanted to do was to get into the Uncle Sam costume his mother wanted him to wear. Twisting loose from her hand, he suddenly fell to the ground in a tantrum. "I ain't goin' to wear that costume. I ain't goin' to do it."

Sadie looked down in distress at her son rolling on the ground as Ben grabbed him by one thrashing arm and roughly lifted him to his feet. Shaking him by his shoulders, he said impatiently, "Enough of your fits, young man. Stop that crying and act your age." The tears rolled silently down Roy's grimy cheeks, and he noisily gulped down his sobs.

"But I don't like that costume," the little boy dared to say.

"Well, I can't imagine why," Ben said brightly. "It's an honor for you to represent Uncle Sam. Your mother chose you purposely because she knew you would do it so well. I remember when I used to recite readings and poems for people who came to watch the medicine show I joined when I was a young boy. It's great fun to perform for people."

"Maybe for you," Roy muttered.

"Not another word," Ben ordered. "Go with your mother and do as she says or you will have me to answer to, and it won't be just a shaking next time."

Sadie took Roy's hand and instructed Ben as she started off with the two boys, "Call everyone to dinner. I'll get the children ready for the skit while people are eating. Get Mardee to help with the serving."

Ben watched his stubborn young son as he left with his mother. He's a strong minded one for a little guy, he thought as a slight smile tugged at his mouth. And a good marble player, too!

Ben made his way to the group listening to the music and announced loudly, "Beans are on the table, folks!"

As people started to meander toward the food, Ben headed over to the shade of a large juniper tree where his 17 year old daughter, Mardee, stood conversing with Judge Corbin. Mardee was a striking girl with the hair and face of an angel, but Ben knew her actions were not always angelic. The judge was leaning lazily against the aged trunk of the tree, smiling down into the eyes of his companion as the sun glinted off his dark blonde hair and reddish-gold mustache. The girl's arms clung to a low limb as she pulled herself up taller than her actual height and stood riveted to his gaze in rapt attention.

"Excuse me, Judge," Ben Spencer quietly interrupted. "Sadie says it's time to eat. As our special guest of honor, you will lead the line to the table. Mardee and I, we will escort our special guest."

Ben took his daughter by the arm and gently maneuvered her around to his right side, and the judge walked on his left. Mardee caught her father's eye and playfully whispered, "I could have escorted the judge myself, you know."

"You are helping to do just that, my dear," was his answer, inaudible to all ears but hers.

Mardee tossed back her mane of bright tousled curls and addressed her father in a rich clear voice, "Papa, you must hear this news. Judge Corbin wants me to come to Santa Fe, and he will speak to Governor McDonald about giving me a job in his office as an interpreter. What do you think of that, Papa?" Her dimpled smile flashed from her father to the judge.

"You do speak Spanish fluently," Ben replied thoughtfully. "But Sadie would be lost without your help. She's a busy woman with the children, the post office, and her teaching duties. We'll have to think about the judge's kind offer, though," Ben said as he dismissed the possibility of his daughter leaving home in the near future. "For right now, you will preside at the table and assist with the serving."

Everyone was seated at the tables and enjoying the delicious food by the time Sadie brought the children out for their skit. Since she was the teacher in the one-room school, she had written a play briefly summarizing the history of the United States to the present time. She was determined that this statehood celebration would be one the children would always remember because of their participation.

George Washington stepped up on an empty table to begin the program. Ben and Sadie's oldest son, Floyd, a gangly teenager, wore a white wig and narrated the events that led to the hard-won freedom of the thirteen colonies from England. George Washington was then joined by Thomas Jefferson, who held a pen and enumerated the struggles of the Constitutional Convention when they framed the important document that formed the foundation for the new country. Ben and Sadie's second son, Charlie, got through his part of the skit, and both boys stepped quickly down with obvious relief.

The third Spencer boy, John, a tall dark-haired young man, dutifully came next and recited the Gettysberg Address. He delivered it brilliantly, concluding with a brief statement that Lincoln had kept the country from division, thus insuring its strength. He jumped lithely off the table after his discourse and smiled at his mother. He knew she was happy he had done so well.

Two Spanish children, Rosa and Rolando Pena, needed help in getting up on the table in their brightly colored full skirts. After Floyd and John had quickly lifted them up, they told of the Spanish Conquistadores who came from Mexico to claim the arid southwestern land for Spain. Then they described the adventures of the Spanish colonists who came up the Rio Grande to build their adobe homes and farm the fertile river soil. "Our ancestors have been here a very long time," they chorused at the end. "We are very proud of them, and we are also proud to be American citizens now." Their large dark eyes and wide smiles expressed relief in finishing their recitations. The boys lifted them off the table and helped two Tompkins children and two Mason children, all in pioneer garb, up for their part of the program.

These children took turns telling in singsong voices of the hardships of traveling west to settle the new land which had been added to the United States after the Mexican War. This group finished their part by singing *Skip to my Lou* and dancing a few careful steps on the table. They started giggling when they finished and, losing their balance, fell into the arms of the Spencer boys.

Now it was time for Uncle Sam, dressed in a beautiful red, white, and blue suit ordered from Albuquerque, to welcome the new state into the Union. Sadie was feeling very pleased with the program, and she pushed little Roy forward to finish it off. He avoided his brothers and quickly scrambled up on the table himself and looked nervously at the crowd. There were a few snickers because he looked so serious, and Roy thought, I knew they would laugh at me in this costume.

Sadie then gave the cue and Roy started reciting his address flawlessly, but in contrast to the fine words he was speaking, he did so with a pouty sullen expression, and the audience reacted with laughter.

Roy wanted to jump off the table and run as far away as his legs would take him, but his father was standing nearby with alert eyes fixed on him in a warning look, so he finished his oration as his face got redder and redder, and he felt angrier and angrier. He received a roaring ovation, and when he turned and climbed down from the table, Ben grinned and said to the crowd, "I hope the Union likes us better than Uncle Sam does!"

Judge Corbin was next, and as he stood before the group of elated New Mexico citizens still laughing from "Uncle Sam's" performance, he said, "After that wonderful entertainment, I don't know who is going to want to listen to me. I am completely upstaged by your young son, Ben!"

Judge Corbin then thanked Sadie for her work on the program and began. "My fellow New Mexico citizens," he said in an eloquent voice, "New Mexico has fought long and hard to achieve acceptance. This state's quest for statehood has been sponsored by important names in the history of the state, names like Catron, Ross, Fall, Andrews, McDonald, Baca, Curry, Fergusson, Luna, and added to that list, many people on the local level like all of you. For example, I have attended many statehood meetings with Ben Spencer.

"It has been almost sixty-four years since the signing of the Treaty of Guadalupe Hidalgo at the end of the Mexican War. The United States is fortunate to have acquired the vast territory of New Mexico and all its outstanding citizens."

As the judge's words rang out Sadie ushered the children into the house to change out of their costumes. She tossed her head and sniffed as she thought, No one is lucky to acquire this Godforsaken land of harsh elements and uncivilized people!

"Roy, you didn't act like a very grateful American citizen of the new state of New Mexico today," Sadie said to the pouty looking little boy scrunched in a big rocking chair as she entered the room. "You will listen to two chapters in the Bible tonight, and then you will be quizzed on them as many times as it takes for you to know what's there. Maybe you will learn to be a respectful son and citizen."

Sadie then sent Roy to change, and she sat in the rocking chair while she waited for the children in the bedrooms to come out. Many times she had sat here and wondered why she had ever left her home in Kansas.

Sarah Adkins had started out to California as a young schoolteacher, working her way west. She had qualified for a job in the Harvey House in Albuquerque and had promised herself she would work there until she had enough money to go on. But she would never go on because Ben Spencer enticed her to the Eastview Community to teach in the school he had provided for his sawmill workers' children.

Sadie slowly shook her head as she remembered. He had done more than just give her a job; he gave her his name and four sons. She had worked hard ever since as wife, mother, teacher, and postmistress in this unyielding frontier land. She knew it had been a marriage of convenience for both of them. She was twenty-eight years old and was aware that if she didn't accept this man's proposal, she would probably never marry. Ben was forty-five years old and had been left with a young daughter to rear when his first wife ran off with one of his sawmill employees. He needed a wife for himself and a mother for Mardee.

This was not a passionate love marriage, but both partners respected each other, and a certain fondness had developed between them. She really never understood her charismatic and ambitious husband, and she never got past the formal speaking stage with him. She usually called him Mr. Spencer, and only in rare warmer moments she called him just Spencer.

Sadie admired Ben and knew he was the undisputed leader of the community. He planned political meetings, dances, picnics, and fiestas. He also welcomed traveling preachers who wandered into the mountains "looking for bed and bread, along with souls," he said. He didn't attend their meetings himself, but he encouraged everyone else, including his wife, to attend. Sadie had been very impressed with these men who carried the message for which her soul hungered.

Sadie remembered becoming a convert, first to the Baptist Church, and then later she became more impressed with a "Hellfire and Damnation" preacher and joined his Holiness Church. This church condemned cursing, gambling, horseracing, and dancing, all activities of which Ben was guilty, Sadie knew, and she gave him many lectures for the sinful life he led. I'm afraid he's too old to change, she thought.

He still continued the life he had always pursued. He sparked his conversations with colorful language, bought good blooded racehorses and bet on their races, and he went to dances on Saturday nights while Sadie stayed home; she went to church on Sundays, and Ben stayed home. It's a 'never the twain shall meet marriage,' she thought shaking her head, but it does seem to persevere.

The children soon trooped out of the bedrooms eager to get back to their outdoor games. Sadie motioned Roy to the stool at her feet as she reached for her Bible.

2

The sun was slowly disappearing behind the Manzanos, and the statehood festivities were winding down. "Good party, Ben," Old Lou Tompkins rasped in his scratchy Texas twang as he sat down with a sigh beside Ben on a rough wooden bench. "Good food," he continued. "Sadie sets a mighty fine table. And the judge made a good speech. Leastways, he's a Republican, so that helps. And that was quite a race yore Diablo horse run."

"He's a fine horse," Ben replied, fixing his old friend with an affectionate grin. "I made a lucky buy when I bought him from the Steeldust Breeders in Texas. He's the first horse of that breed in Torrance County, and none of the other horses can touch him, especially with that boy of mine riding him. He's quite a rider, don't you think?"

"Floyd was born fer the saddle. He sticks thar like a danged burr," Old Lou retorted admiringly. "He and that big Steeldust hoss make a handsome pair." He jingled the money in his faded overall pocket. "Made me some extra silver dollars on that race," he confided smugly.

"Fine!" Ben remarked, and patting his jacket pocket said, "I did all right, too, but don't tell Sadie. She'll report me to the preacher!"

"Don't worry," said Old Lou, "I don't talk to preacher mans or to priest mans. That priest man at Punta thinks ever'one should bow to him when he walks by. He told me to take off my hat and bow, and I hit him right on his holy nose and laid him out flat. I guess I don't stand a chance o' getting prayed into heaven now, but I ain't a'feared. Course, my Indian wife is mad as a tarpin at me. That religion man has caused me a world o' trouble."

"Too bad," said Ben sympathetically, "but you better stay away from the

Father, Louie. He's got his followers and admirers around here. They don't take kindly to someone attacking their priest." To change the subject, Ben added, "By the way, what did you think of the footrace?"

The scowl on Old Lou's face was replaced with a smile. "That was a fine race, Ben. Yore boy, Charlie, is quite a runner." Old Lou knew Ben liked for people to brag on his sons.

"Oh yes," the proud father agreed. "You know I'm taking him to Oklahoma City later this summer to compete in the National Footracing Championships, don't you?"

"Yup, he'll whup 'em good," Old Lou prophesied. "He growed up runnin' over these mountains, and he's got strong lungs and legs." He spat an accurate stream of tobacco juice on a raspberry plant a few feet away for emphasis.

Ben smiled vaguely at his old friend, only partially listening, and paying more attention to the scene around them. The musicians played on vigorously as the dancers whirled to the strains of oldtime fiddle breakdowns like *Turkey in the Straw* and *Golden Slippers*. Occasionally New Mexico Spanish music would slip in with songs like *Ya no Sopla* and *La Cucaracha*. That young fellow, Kurt, is quite a fiddler, Ben thought. He marveled at the lovely notes produced with a seemingly magic bow.

Kurt was part of the Mason clan who were neighbors to the Spencers. They had come to the Manzano hills after the Spencers and were also in the sawmill business.

Kurt Mason was a gentle artistic young man whose music was his main interest in life. He had been known to be the cause of the whole school playing hookey as the students slipped off into the woods to dance to his fiddle rather than pursue their book learning. Kurt had picked up his music from the oldtime fiddlers, both Anglo and Spanish, but had added to the traditional breakdowns and the lilting Spanish music by composing his own original music which almost reproduced the sound of some of the Old World composers. His original composition of the *Manzano Melody* had a hint of the beautiful sound of *The Blue Danube Waltz*. His Austrian ancestors had passed on their love of music to him, and the peaceful mountain setting in which he lived inspired his ability. He had no musical training, just outstanding raw talent. He had been playing music for all the community celebrations for several years now although he was only eighteen years old.

Kurt had just closed his eyes and drawn his bow expertly over the strings of his violin as the sun was disappearing in a last blast of muted redness behind the mountains. Bonnets were being cast aside as couples enjoyed the coolness of the evening, and they stamped their feet and moved in joyful rhythmic steps.

Kurt finished a Spanish waltz, *The Pike's Peak Waltz*, so-named because an old Spaniard they called Pike played it, and started into the catchy strains of *Put Your Little Foot*. Ben watched Mardee as she danced the intricate steps perfectly and gracefully with her athletic partner, Judge Corbin. The young girl's face was flushed with excitement as the handsome lawyer twirled her around in perfect time to the music. Her curls tumbled in chaotic profusion around her delicately molded facial features. So beautiful and so full of life, but so naive, her father worried to himself. What will happen to her in this wild country?

Ben's young daughter was obviously enchanted with Jeff Corbin, and Jeff was charmed with her, but Ben knew there existed an agreement between Jeff and the lieutenent governor that Jeff would marry his daughter when she returned from school in the East. That was the main reason the young Socorro lawyer had received his appointment to work in the new state government. Now Jeff wanted Mardee to go to Santa Fe and work close to him. That was not a good idea, and Ben shook his head as he pondered. Mardee is infatuated with the dashing young lawyer, but she is too inexperienced in the romance department to be on her own with him in Santa Fe, Ben told himself.

Ben was brought back to attention when he heard Old Lou say, "What you a'shakin' yorn head about, Ben? I jest said I was a'goin' to have to whup that young squaw o' mine and all those kids if she didn't start getting more work done in the fields, and I'll do it, Ben. You know I will. We got to have enough beans for winter."

"I know, I know," Ben said as he patted Old Lou's scrawny knee. His friend ran his household with his own unique rules. He was the total ruler, and if wife and children didn't conform to his wishes at all times, he whipped them with a horse whip. He was on his fourth wife; the others had died or run away. He had secured a young woman from the Isleta Pueblo over by Albuquerque after he lost his last wife. She had given him trouble from the beginning by insisting on being married by the priest at Punta de Agua, and Old Lou didn't believe in that "religious stuff." But he wanted the woman pretty badly, so he had given in to the priest's marrying them, not realizing that the woman would also want to go to church, and then she had been determined to have the babies baptized. She was a strong Indian woman whom the old man needed to work his fields and tend his children, but his patience was growing more and more strained.

Ben turned full attention to his friend. "I wouldn't do that, Louie. This woman might not take kindly to beatings. Maybe she's the kind that a little good treatment would produce better results than the whip."

"I does what I has to do," Old Lou announced firmly, setting his skinny jaw in a straight line. Ben knew there was no use in talking any more on this subject. Old Lou Tompkins was a tough old man. He had been run out of Texas "because I was a Republican," so he said, but Ben suspected there was more to the story. Anyway, he had evaded a posse and their bloodhounds by wading and swimming up the Brazos River and then heading north until he crossed the state line. He hadn't stopped running until he got to the Manzano Mountains where he felt safe at last. He had homesteaded 160 acres of mountain land, taken a Mexican girl for a wife, and started raising beans and kids. He was a hard man, but Ben had found him to be totally honest and a good loyal friend. He knew Louie Tompkins would lay down his life anytime for Ben Spencer.

Suddenly a shot split the night air, followed by a woman's scream. Ben jumped to his feet, drew his gun, and was striding toward the dancers in one quick movement. As the couples edged back in the dim light, Ben saw a man on a horse in the middle of the dancers. He was swinging a gun above his head, and another shot went off as he yelled, "Viva Nuevo Mejico!"

"A drunk statehood celebrant," Ben muttered as he leaped forward. Grabbing the bridle of the horse, he leveled his .45 caliber gun at the intruder and spoke in a firm steady voice, "Give me that gun, you crazy bastard, or I'll blow your drunken head off."

The rider looked down at Ben Spencer, and his befuddled brain tried to assimilate the ultimatum he'd just been given. Even in his fogged state of mind he was aware that he should pay attention to this man, but his brain was in no condition to give any quick signals, so he still brandished the gun over his head. At that moment, before Ben followed through on his threat, Mardee appeared at her father's side, speaking with quiet urgency. "Papa, it's only Frankie Moseby. He won't hurt anyone. Let me talk to him."

Ben pushed Mardee roughly back. "Get out of the way," he ordered, and in the same breath continued, "Frankie, give me that gun."

Frankie's eyes were on Mardee. Slowly his hand came down, and turning the gun, handle first toward Mardee, he said, "Si, Senor Spencer. I give the gun to Mardita. Take it, mi hita."

Mardee took one step forward, her eyes fastened on the horseman's face, and reached for his gun, but Ben's gun smashed down with lightning force, sending the gun careening away from both Frankie and Mardee. "Stay away from my daughter, hombre, entiendes? Get the hell out of here--NOW! AHORA! VAMOS! COMPRENDES? ANDALE!" He slapped the horse on the rear, and the rider was gone as fast as he had come.

Ben stood silently in the middle of the dancers for a long second. He then picked up the gun and handed it to Floyd who had come up beside him during the ruckus. "Take it to the house. We'll keep it until he is in better shape to get it back."

Turning to Mardee he said, "Tell Judge Corbin goodnight. It's time for you to go in, too." Addressing the musicians, he said, "Good job, boys. Play *Home Sweet Home*, Kurt. It's been an inspiring day, but we must now call a halt to the festivities." And with a rueful grin, he raised his arm and proclaimed loudly, "Viva, Nuevo Mejico!"

3

Ben escorted Jeff Corbin up the stairs to the guest bedroom. Sadie followed them bringing a pitcher of hot water and towels so their guest could freshen up before retiring. Ben waited for Sadie to place the pitcher and towels near an earthenware basin on a wooden chest and say goodnight, and as she closed the door behind her, he turned to his friend. "Jeff, I appreciate your telling me about the new bank John Becker is planning to build in Belen. I'll get right over to see him about furnishing the lumber. I'm glad to hear he's expanding."

Jeff took off his leather vest and laid it across a chair and sat down on the end of the bed. It had been a long ride the day before to get to Eastview for the celebration, and he had a long ride back to Belen the next morning so he could catch a train for Santa Fe. "I wanted to tell you about this project before anyone else knew about it, Ben," he said. "I know the Masons will be interested in the job, but I'd like to see you get it. I'm sure you could handle it. And you have a reputation for good lumber. You made quite a name for yourself when you got the bid to provide the lumber for the ties and timber for the bridges to bring the Santa Fe Railroad across the mountains. I'd be happy to put in a good word for you with John Becker."

"I appreciate that, Jeff, but I know John well. We've done business together ever since I came here in '87. You know, he did banking business in his mercantile store for many years, and then I furnished the lumber for the first small bank he built in 1904. So we've been business associates and friends for a long time. But again, I appreciate your telling me about his new endeavor."

Ben started out of the room and paused to say, "Sadie will have breakfast for you in the morning, and she will make you up a pack of food to tide you over on your long ride." He hesitated for a few moments. "Thanks for the job offer for Mardee. She's young, though, and probably should stay home a while longer. She's only seventeen, and as I said, Sadie needs her right now. She's a bright girl, though, and the time may come when I want her to get more education, and maybe she could work and go to school in Santa Fe. We'll talk about this at a later date."

"Just let me know, and I will be happy to be of help to her," Jeff replied. The two men shook hands, the ambitious young lawyer and the pioneer business man. Each felt respect for the other, but each understood the other's motives perhaps only too well.

Ben then joined Sadie in the kitchen where she was preparing the starter for her breakfast sourdough hot cakes. This was the first time during this long day that there was an opportunity for talk between the two. "Thanks for all your help today," Ben remarked. "You did a good job. The food was plentiful and delicious, and the children's skit was very good. Roy's Uncle Sam character was hilarious." Ben threw back his head and laughed.

"I'd prefer that you not laugh at that kind of behavior," Sadie retorted icily. "The boy was punished for his attitude, and I do not want you making light of his misdeeds in his presence."

Ben enjoyed teasing his sober wife, but he knew he had now gone far enough. "Don't worry, Sadie," he said soothingly. However, in his mind he was thinking that because of Roy's rebellion a little humor had been added to an otherwise too serious skit, so in his opinion, this had made the program better. But he knew he should not voice his thoughts.

With Ben in a good mood, Sadie decided to bring up the subject of Mardee. She was beginning to worry about the pretty girl who was starting to cast flirtatious eyes at the sawmill workers. "I must tell you something else that is on my mind, Mr. Spencer," she continued. "Mardee is a born flirt, and she is beginning to pay too much attention to all the men, young or old, Spanish or Anglo. That Frankie Moseby hangs around her every chance he gets. They were friends at school, and he was a nice boy and a smart one, but he's starting to drink just like his Mexican mother, and he can't handle liquor. Why do you suppose he came riding in crazy drunk tonight? To get a glimpse of Mardee, of course. I know Mardee is the apple of your eye, but you have to be more strict with her. Instead of all this dancing she should be going to church, but if you don't go, how can I make her go?" She turned away with a disgusted sigh.

Church, he thought. All their discussions inevitably ended up with her disappointment over what she perceived as his lack of religion. He knew he was actually a very deeply spiritual man inside, but his wife didn't understand his way of religion. And he knew she was right about his high-spirited daughter. He made a mental note that he must do something about that young stallion, Frankie .

"You're right, Sadie, as always. I'll see what I can do. It's been a long day, my dear. It's time for bed."

4

Jeff pushed back his chair, thanked Sadie for the breakfast, and headed for the door. "I must go, Ben," he said, taking his hat and jacket from the coat rack. "It's been good seeing you again, but I've got to get on my way."

Ben followed his guest to the door with Mardee close behind. "Thank you for your visit and your participation in our celebration. You have a lot of support around here if you ever need it in the future," Ben said, with a wink. "Your horse is saddled, and Sadie has some food for you."

"Here are some bacon and egg sandwiches and some cinnamon rolls," Sadie said as she handed him a neatly tied bag. "You have a long ride ahead of you. Maybe this will tide you over."

Jeff took the bag with one hand and Sadie's hand with the other. "Thank you so much, Mrs. Spencer. That's going to taste mighty good on the trail." Raising her hand, he kissed the workworn fingers. Sadie's face reddened, and she drew her hand back abruptly and jammed it into her apron pocket, returning quickly to the table as a nervous hum escaped her throat.

Ben shook hands with Jeff Corbin and wished him well on his new job. Jeff smiled at Mardee and started to say goodbye, but she pushed past her father and the judge. "I'm going to ride to the main road with Jeff, Papa. All right?" Mardee looked anxiously at her father who nodded his affirmation. Then her stepmother's head appeared at Ben's shoulder. The face that had been almost girlish a moment before was now cold and reproachful.

"Don't linger long, Missy," she instructed. "You must get the morning chores done. I will be in the post office all day."

"I'll be back, Mother Spencer," Mardee replied impatiently. Walking beside Jeff to his horse, she said in a low voice, "I hate her. Someday I'll get away."

Jeff looked down at the girl by his side. Her auburn hair shone in the morning sun, and her bluish-green eyes blazed rebellion through angry tears. "It's all right, Mardee. Sadie just doesn't have time to understand a girl like you."

"No, she doesn't," Mardee said with quiet intensity. "She has never been young and in love. Jeff, take me with you. You said you'd help me get a job." She looked up at him with imploring eyes.

"We'll talk about this as we ride along," Jeff said softly. "Is that your horse?" He pointed to a mare standing beside his big sorrel.

"Yes, this is Gypsy," Mardee said over her shoulder as she ran and put her arms lovingly around the horse's neck. The chestnut turned her proud head trustingly toward her mistress. "She can run, too. She can beat Papa's Diablo horse in a short race, even though he won't admit it."

Jeff could tell by looking at the animal's muscled chest and legs that she could run. Fine blooded horse and girl, he thought admiringly. He knew these two beauties were perfectly suited for each other.

Mardee sprang easily into the saddle in spite of her voluminous skirts and settled into her western saddle comfortably. She had never ridden side saddle. "I would race you to the road," she challenged merrily, "if I didn't want this ride to last as long as possible."

Once out of sight of the house the riders pulled their horses close together. Mardee held her reins lightly with her left hand and put her right hand over on Jeff's shoulder. Jeff was thoughtful as he debated in his mind how to handle this impetuous girl. He found her very tempting, but there were complications right now. Given time, he would try to work them out, but for the present he had a new job and another girl to whom he had responsibilities. Ben did not want his daughter leaving home right now, anyway, so he had some time to figure out his dilemma.

Jeff was a man who had always known what he wanted and had usually been able to accomplish his goals. He had left the grinding work of his father's

Kansas homestead and had gotten an education in Wichita. With law degree in hand he had headed west over the Santa Fe Trail in search of virgin country and interesting opportunities.

In Santa Fe Jeff studied the geography of the territory and decided to head down El Camino Real to the flourishing communities on the Rio Grande. He passed through Albuquerque and Belen to Socorro which had been settled by the Spanish in the 1600's and was now a hub for settlers coming from Texas and Mexico, as well as those coming from the east going to California.

Here he established his office, the first "Gringo" to practice law in the area. He was twenty-six years old and truly liked the people who were a mixture of Spanish, Indian, and Texan. His easy friendliness and genuine concern to do a good job soon earned him acceptance with everyone, and he was elected judge of the district. He ate cornbread and beans with the Anglo citizens and tortillas and beans with the darker ones. He attended the square dances and fiestas of each group, but he found no romantic interest kindled in him by the shy uneducated pioneer girls or the more spirited senoritas.

Jeff had met Ben Spencer at a statehood meeting in Belen and had been intrigued with the pretty daughter who accompanied her father. Although only sixteen years old, she had done a commendable job of interpreting for the Spanish speaking participants at the meeting. She had more poise and self-confidence than Jeff expected from one who had been raised on a ranch in the eastern foothills of the Manzano Mountains.

Ben and Jeff had liked each other immediately and had joined efforts to gain statehood for their territory. The younger man admired the older man's good judgment and clear thinking, and the mature man saw in Jeff many of the qualities that had always dominated his life's actions. He knew instinctively that Jeff was a leader of the future, one who would help form the profile of the new land. Each man appreciated the other, and each learned from the other. It was inevitable that their paths would intertwine.

For the last year Jeff had found reasons to come to the Spencer Ranch at least once every two months. Jeff had cases in Mountainair, and on his way back he would stop at the Spencer Ranch to stay overnight.

Ben was only part of the attraction. Jeff was fascinated as he watched Mardee develop into a striking young woman. She was unspoiled, unaffected and beautiful. Her wavy auburn hair caught the fire of the sun and framed to perfection her wideset turquoise eyes and vibrant lips--eyes and lips that could drive a man to distraction.

Mardee's stepmother had given her a good education, and she had also taught her to be charming and well mannered. She could act like a refined lady which was rare in this raw land. But she had her father's independence, and she would occasionally show the exuberance of her personality and a determination to be her own person. Ben loved her more than anyone in the world, but he knew when she set her pretty head in dead earnest it was hard to rein her in. Jeff had watched their deadlocked struggles with interest, feeling loyalty to each, and realizing that Mardee, in spite of her tender years, was the first western girl to really hold his interest.

As Jeff and Ben continued working with those who wanted statehood for New Mexico, they eventually met with all the influential leaders of this prospective state. One gentleman, William McDonald, was recognized as the man with the background to be the first governor. He had come to White Oaks, New Mexico, in 1880 and had become a leading citizen in this mushrooming mining town. He was a lawyer and an engineer and had used his expertise in the mines as well as the ranching community.

Ben had done business with William McDonald when he operated his sawmill in the White Oaks area before he came to the Manzanos, and he knew him to be an extremely honest, bright, ambitious, and fair man. He felt sure he would give New Mexico the leadership it needed in its formative statehood years, so Ben threw his support behind him and influenced Jeff to do the same. Likewise, McDonald courted the favor of Ben and Jeff, knowing both men would be valuable to him in the future. The prospective governor wanted the brains of young men like Jeff Corbin and the vision of influential men like Ben Spencer to help him run the government of the new state. They also understood the natives and got along well with them, so McDonald knew he could trust their judgment and advice in this area.

The prospective lieutenant governor had also noticed Jeff. Although he knew this young state would be good for his political future, he worried about Heather, his only child. The prospect of her finding a suitable mate in this farflung frontier land was dim. With the governor's help he arranged for the two young people to meet, and he subtly let Jeff know his wishes for their marital future. He pointed out that he would be the natural heir to the Governor's Palace after McDonald's occupancy, and Jeff would be assured of a good appointment.

Jeff was flattered, and he appeared to agree with these plans. Heather had gone back to school in the east; so there would be no necessity for a definite commitment for some time. He had found Heather somewhat attractive and appealing, but he knew he had stronger feelings for Mardee. The girl from the mountains was too entrenched in his mind and heart to seriously consider anyone else right now. But deep inside himself he knew instictively that Heather, rather than Mardee, was the girl in his future.

Mardee interrupted Jeff's thoughts as she suddenly slid off her horse and tied the reins to a low hanging cedar branch. Jeff reined in his horse and joined her. She cradled his face with her hands. "Jeff, do be careful," she implored. "You're going to have to camp out tonight, and there are Indians and outlaws hiding out in the bosque along the river." She held him tighter. "You know, when Papa had his mill in White Oaks in Lincoln County he had to bank in Santa Fe, so he went there occasionally to do his business. It was a three-day ride. On one trip he had made camp the first night and had just finished his supper when a rider suddenly rode up from out of nowhere. Papa invited him to have some food. The man accepted the beans and biscuits my father dug out of his knapsack, wolfing down the food and barely answering questions Papa put to him.

"Because he seemed so hungry Papa gave him more food, but the stranger wrapped it in his bandanna, swiftly mounted his horse, and was gone as fast as he had come without as much as a 'thank you.' Papa said there was something different about this man. He wore no coat even though it was cool in the mountains. As he faded into the shadows of the chilly night, Papa mulled over the stories he had heard of the desperado, William Bonney, who never wore a coat on the theory that it might interfere with his ability to speedily draw his pistol if the need arose. 'But surely this skinny hungry waif is not the illustrious outlaw,' Papa concluded.

"A few months later," Mardee continued, "Papa saw the same man gun down someone in a bar in White Oaks. Papa and another man were having a drink in the bar when a third man came in and stood at the bar beside Papa's drinking friend. 'I'll buy you a drink,' the newcomer said.

"'No, you won't,' retorted the man standing beside Papa.

"'I said I'd buy you a drink,' the man repeated slowly. 'Maybe you didn't understand me the first time.'

"'I understood you perfectly. I won't drink with a killer.' The words came out flat and hostile and final." Mardee shivered with excitement.

"There were no more words spoken," she continued. "The man who offered the drink backed up, pulled his gun, and shot the one who would not drink with him point-blank in the heart. The victim slumped over the bar and fell to the floor as the killer backed out swiftly, his gun trained on the stunned audience. When he got to the door he turned and made a running jump on his horse and was gone in a cloud of dust. Papa said to the bartender, 'Who was that? We'd better go after him.'

"But the bartender replied, 'That's Billy the Kid, and no, we won't be going after him.'"

Mardee's eyes were wide with the memory of her father's encounters with this young desperado. "Then Papa knew who his visitor in the mountains had been. And he knew that if Billy the Kid had ever reached in his knapsack and found the money he carried under the food, he probably would have been a dead man, also. He was sure he would have been killed in cold blood. But maybe not." Mardee paused and squared her pretty jaw. "Papa is very good with his gun, and he can draw as fast and shoot as straight as any man in the West. But anyway, as I was saying, you must be careful on your trip."

Jeff pulled Mardee closer into his arms. He smiled tenderly down into her worried face. "Don't worry, my little wildwood flower. Billy the Kid lies moldering in his grave, and his men are scattered to the four winds. I'll have a good trip through the mountains, and I'll have sweet dreams of the prettiest girl in the West," he said softly as his searching lips drank in the sweet innocence of her young yearnings.

When he released her she leaned against his chest. "I want to go with you," she sobbed. "I can't stay here, Jeff. I want to get out of this prison." Her small fists beat lightly against his chest like a bird fluttering at the bars of its cage. "Say you'll help me."

Jeff's heart ached at the desperation in her voice. "I'll need some time, little one. But I'll help you, I promise. I'll make things work out for you. In the meantime, carry on with life as usual. Be patient, and someday you'll see the lights of Santa Fe." He kissed her pouty mouth and stroked her wet cheeks. "Don't be sad, my pretty one. I need a smile before I go."

Mardee took a deep breath, mustered a smile, and clung to him tightly one more time. He kissed her gently this time, loosened her arms, and mounted his horse. With a last smile and a wave he jabbed his spurs into his horse's flanks.

Mardee watched until he disappeared in the distance. Then she walked over to her horse and put her arms around Gypsy's neck as sobs shook her slender body like an autumn wind attacking the delicate golden leaves of a mountain aspen tree.

5

Just within sight of the house Mardee stopped under a large yellow pine tree. "I need to visit Grammy," she told Gypsy as she eased down, tied her to a low branch, and fell in a heap on her grandmother's grave.

Elizabeth Spencer and her son, Ben, had headed west after her husband had died in Illinois. Ben was sixteen years old and a man already under his new responsibilities. They bought a home in Dodge City, Kansas, and after Ben had hunted buffalo, traveled with a circus and a medicine show, and worked in a sawmill, they sold the home and bought the sawmill as Ben had found he loved to work with machinery. They joined the land rush to Oklahoma, knowing that in that awakening country lumber would be in demand.

But timber was scarce, and they had to move often to find new sources. They soon headed for the forested mountains of New Mexico, moving the sawmill equipment on heavy wagons pulled by oxen. They also carried an extra passenger. Ben had been smitten by an appealing half Cherokee Indian girl, so his pregnant wife, Zada, accompanied Ben and his mother and all their worldly goods. They settled in the heavily timbered Sacramento Mountains of southern New Mexico and set up a mill near the mining town of White Oaks.

Lumber was easy to produce here, but the demand for it soon dwindled. The boom town days of White Oaks were slowing down, and within a few years when the railroad opted to bypass the mining town, the thriving town of Carrizozo sprang up and ultimately bugled the requiem for White Oaks.

Ben had heard of mountains to the south of Albuquerque that had good timber and were on the outskirts of many settlements. The Spanish explorers had passed near this area in the 17th century searching for the fabled Seven Cities of Gold. Into the foothills of these mountains the Spanish priests had come, building missions and teaching the native Indians to farm, to live in adobe and rock houses, and to worship the white man's God. An apple orchard planted on an early Spanish Land Grant still survived near the mountain town of Manzano. This orchard probably accounted for the name of the mountains, Manzano (Apple) Mountains. Ben Spencer decided this would be a good home for his family, and again he packed up his mill machinery on heavy wagons and moved.

The Indians had all left the area by the time the Spencers moved to this frontier, but the descendants of Spanish explorers were thickly settled in the mountain villages of Abo, Punta de Agua, Manzano, Torreon, Escabosa, Tajique, and Chilili. The Spencers were the only family there who were not of Spanish descent.

Ben had what he needed here for a successful business. Albuquerque was a fast growing town only 60 miles over the mountains. New settlers were flocking to the Rio Grande Valley, homesteading the land and building homes. There was adequate cheap labor in the villages, so Ben homesteaded 160 acres in Barranca Canyon where there was water, and the mountains soon echoed to the axes and saws of the Spencer Lumber Company.

Ben's business went well, but his personal life hit a snag. His pretty wife, Zada, was not content as a wife and mother. The household chores she found uninteresting, and being a mother she found tiresome. Ben's mother did everything, anyway, since the young wife didn't know how to cook what Ben liked or how to keep the house the way he preferred. The grandmother also knew how to take care of the baby better than the mother, so the frustrated pioneer wife started looking around for something to fulfill her life.

She found it in a young sawyer who worked in the mill. The two left together while Ben was in Albuquerque with a load of lumber. He came home with a good price for his lumber, but found no wife or sawyer. However, he was not surprised. He had known his wife was unhappy, and he was too busy to try to make things better for her. The initial attraction they had felt for each other had quickly worn off, and each realized the other was not the right mate. His mother would take care of the baby, and he was now free to devote all his time to his business. Ben even contracted with the Gross Kelly Lumber Company and sold lumber as far north as Santa Fe.

Elizabeth Spencer and her spirited little granddaughter, Mardee, had loved each other with a passion. Mardee brightened the hard life of the older woman, and she gave her "Little Hummingbird," as she called her, all the love and security she needed. Mardee talked and sang and danced and was perpetual movement in her grandmother's life. One night after she had danced around the room singing a song and had fluttered onto the lap of her grandmother, covering her face with kisses, Elizabeth remarked with a laugh, "You're just like a little hummingbird."

"What's a hummingbird, Grammy?" the pretty child demanded.

"A bright colored little bird that whirs through the air looking for honey, just like you," Elizabeth laughingly answered. One of her favorite things in Kansas had been watching the hummingbirds visit her sweetpeas for honey.

"What color is it?" Mardee persisted.

"Red and blue-green and honey colored just like you," Elizabeth fondly replied, kissing her tousled curls. "I haven't seen any hummingbirds in the Manzanos, but I have my Mardeebird."

"And I have my Grammy," Mardee said happily. She had never missed her mother because she had always had her Grammy.

Mardee had been four years old when Ben married Sarah Adkins, and she had taken an instant dislike to this new woman in her life. She resented the attention her father gave to his new bride, and she instinctively knew the prim lady did not like her. She made her pick up her things, talk softly, and lectured her unendingly. Her grandmother told her quietly to do what Sadie said, but not to worry since Grammy would always be there to take care of her. And Grammy was there for her, even when other babies started coming at regular intervals. Four sons joined the family: Floyd, Charlie, John, and Roy. And Mardeebird loved her little brothers as deeply as she loved her father and her grandmother.

Overall, Mardee's early life was satisfying and happy, but when she was fourteen years old her world crashed. She and Sadie and the older boys came home from school one day to find her grandmother lying quietly on the bed. Little Roy, the only child not in school, was playing contentedly on the floor with his wooden blocks. Mardee ran to her grandmother to give her a kiss, but she instantly realized something was wrong. Sadie felt her brow and her wrist as a frown creased her face.

"What's wrong, what's wrong?" Mardee shrilled. "Is Grammy sick?"

Sadie turned to Mardee sternly. "Quiet, child. Go fetch your father from the mill. Yes, your grandmother is very sick. Run very fast, child."

Mardee ran the short distance from the house to the mill, her heart beating wildly as silent sobs filled her throat chokingly, and she prayed to the God her stepmother was always talking about, "Please, God, don't let her die. Please, God."

But Elizabeth Spencer was dead. The demanding years of frontier life had taken their toll on her body, and she had known for some time she wasn't well. She knew the high altitude was not good for her heart, but she hadn't complained to Ben. She was buried under a pine tree not too far from the house. For some reason the tall strong tree reminded Ben of his brave little mother.

Sadie told Mardee that her grandmother was now in heaven, but that didn't bring any comfort to her. She was devastated by the sudden loss of her beloved "Grammy," and her carefree childhood was forever buried with her grandmother in the cold grave. Sadie, with her husband's approval, immediately forced Mardee to assume mature responsibilities and help with the children and the household chores. Sadie was an exacting task mistress. She needed a lot of help, and she wanted things done right.

Mardee went about her work in silent resignation, knowing that the little hummingbird her grandmother had talked about now had her wings clipped. I'll never laugh and whir through the air looking for honey again, she thought.

A blue jay was scolding from the pine tree as Mardee raised herself slowly from her grandmother's grave and turned her tearstained face to the mountains that had been her home since she could remember. Unbidden, the words of one of the many Bible verses her stepmother had made her memorize came to her mind: "I will lift up mine eyes to the hills from whence cometh my help." As always, her grandmother had seemed to be there to comfort her. Afterall, hadn't she promised that she would always be with her Mardeebird?

Mardee's lively spirit reasserted itself, and she and Gypsy were quickly on their way across the pasture to the barn. She took off the saddle, gave her horse an affectionate hug and some grain, and hurried to the house. She was late in getting her morning chores started.

Floyd had left a fresh pail of milk on the kitchen table. She put it through the milk separator to remove the cream and then put the milk and cream in the ice house. Then she went to the chicken house. She hated the stupid hens and their noise and flapping and was always relieved to get this chore out of the way.

Mardee carried her basket of eggs back to the kitchen and started to mix the dough for the week's bread. She mixed the dry ingredients in one dishpan and then poured six cups of lukewarm water into another. To the warm water she added two cakes of yeast and some melted lard. To the liquid mixture she started adding the flour mixture, beating thoroughly after each addition until the dough was stiff enough to kneed. She worked the dough with strong hands until it was smooth and elastic, about ten minutes. She knew from the smell and consistency of the dough when it was ready to be put in the other dishpan to rise. She then plumped the large ball of dough into the pan and covered it with a damp warm dishtowel. Now she was ready to tidy up the kitchen, sweep the floors, and make the beds. She worked fast and sang one of the songs her papa loved to sing, *Little Girl Dressed in Blue*. Her stepmother always hummed as she worked, but Mardee sang the words as she worked. She had an excellent ability to memorize the lyrics to verses and songs, and she knew all the songs that Ben and Sadie sang.

On the long summer evenings the family often sat on the porch and sang together. These were the times when she even felt close to Sadie. Sadie sang mostly hymns, but she had a pleasing contralto voice which Mardee appreciated and tried unsuccessfully to duplicate with her young vibrant soprano. Mardee had learned from her stepmother that singing made even the most mundane chores less boring.

With her morning chores done, Mardee always looked forward to the time of day when she would fix a hearty lunch to take to her father at the mill. Along the way she visited with the sawmill workers. She loved the smiles and remarks they directed to her. She had known many of them most of her life. She was a bright spot in their day, and they provided the social companionship she needed. She knew instinctively that some of the younger men were looking at her with more than just a friendly light in their eyes, but with her father around, she knew they wouldn't dare take advantage of the innocent flirting that came naturally with her warm nature.

"Hello, Pedro," she said, flashing her dimpled smile at the edger man. "Como esta?"

Pedro waved and his black eyes sparkled. "Como esta, Mardita. How was the baile? I hear you dance with the judge."

"Si," Mardee laughed merrily, "and with everybody--con todos!" Pedro shook his head in mock shame and went on with his trimming work.

Mardee waved at the men working on the logpile and then headed into the small wooden shack that was her father's office. He sat at his desk pouring over a pile of papers. He looked up as she entered, and his blue eyes brightened with pleasure when he saw her. "Thank God it's you, darlin'!" he announced. "I'm starved, and I can't get these orders straightened out. Look through these papers while I eat and see if you can find an invoice for the Abo Land Company."

Mardee liked to help her father. And she loved the smell of fresh cut lumber which permeated the air, as well as the books and papers with long columns of figures which she could sweep swiftly down with a glance and come up with the right answers. She had inherited her father's quickness for numbers. He had very little formal schooling, but was known as the best mathematician in the country.

Ben started on his lunch which was a headcheese sandwich, two boiled eggs, and a butter and plum jelly sandwich with cool sweet milk from a Mason jar to drink. Mardee quickly went through the stack of invoices, chattering as she looked for the order Ben needed. "How do you stand that headcheese?" she asked, grimacing. "I can still see that horrible hog's head cooking on the stove."

"It's delicious," Ben answered, smacking his lips. "Sadie got just the right seasoning in this batch."

Mardee soon found the missing invoice and placed it on top of the stack of papers with a satisfied sigh. Sitting back in her leather seated chair that creaked as she moved, she looked thoughtfully at her father and said, "Papa, I'm going to miss Jeff. Thank you for letting me ride a ways with him this morning."

"Don't let yourself become too emotionally involved with Jeff for a while," her father counseled. "He is going to be a very busy man for several months. He must work hard to try to do a commendable job for the governor. He's a young man with a minimum of experience for his demanding job. It will be a very challenging time for him, but I'm sure he will be successful in the long run."

"Do you like him, Papa?" Mardee asked, her eyes riveted on her father's face.

"Very much," Ben replied as he took a swallow of milk. "He will make a name for himself in the state of New Mexico in due time. He is a young man with a future."

"Is that future going to include me, Papa?"

"Don't be impatient, my little Mardeebird. You still belong only to me. What would we do without you, darlin'? Here, take half of my sandwich. You helped Sadie make this plum jelly. It is excellent."

Mardee took the sandwich and chewed it slowly, tasting the tartly sweet contents. Yes, it's good, but not as good as a kiss from Jeff, she thought. She didn't dare say as much to her father.

Ben finished the milk, put the lid back on, and brushed the crumbs from his desk. Mardee realized this was her signal to return to the house. She rose reluctantly and looked at her father wistfully. She'd rather stay here with him, but she knew she had to check her bread dough. "I love you, Papa." The words came out unplanned.

Ben raised his eyes from the papers that had already drawn his attention. They softened as he looked deeply into his daughter's beautiful misty blue-green eyes. "I love you, too, darlin'. Yo tengo mucho amor para tu. Comprendes?"

"Si," Mardee replied softly, and then with a giggle she was gone.

6

Mardee's good spirits had returned as she headed to the house. Being with her father always had that effect. When he talked to her, even when he lectured, she felt close to him, and there was never any doubt in her mind that he wanted the best for her. He was the one constant in her life. She had always felt proud to be Ben Spencer's daughter, and she was secure in the knowledge of how special she was to him.

As she walked Mardee started whistling the *Mockingbird* tune Kurt Mason had played on his fiddle. He had made the varied notes of a mockingbird in song emerge from his instrument as he deftly swept the bow over the strings. It was difficult for Mardee to reproduce those notes with her mouth, and as she whistled, getting out some good notes as well as some sour ones, her concert was suddenly interrupted by the raucous squawk of a blackbird. She paused and frowned in the direction of the noise.

Her vexation was replaced by amusement as she heard the blackbird squawks change to laughter. Then she spotted a man standing in the trees. She recognized the broad shoulders and mane of black hair and muttered to herself, "Frankie, you rascal, what are you doing here?"

Frankie waved to her, and she started laughing, enjoying the joke. As she joined her friend, she dissolved into breathless giggles even though she wanted to reprimand him. He took her hands and looked down at her fondly. "I just had to join in your concert, mi hita. Do you laugh at my singing?"

"Frankie, you are such a fooler," Mardee said getting her breath. "I thought there was a blackbird convention going on over here in the trees. What are you doing here?"

Frankie's face darkened as he looked deep into her eyes. "No blackbirds, Mardita, just me coming to tell you goodbye."

"Goodbye? What are you talking about, Frankie?" The roses in her face started to fade.

"It's all right, mi hita." Frankie pulled her closer. "I'm going to Belen to get a job on the railroad. Your father has given me a letter to give to the yardboss there."

Mardee pulled away at the mention of her father. "Papa is sending you to Belen?" Her face turned white.

"Your papa is not happy over the way I acted at the celebration. I don't blame him. I was very stupid, querida. Please forgive me. I would never hurt you, you know that. Tell me, please, that you believe me." Frankie looked contritely into Mardee's eyes.

"Of course, I know that, Frankie," Mardee replied impatiently. "Surely my father doesn't think you are dangerous." But in her mind she knew Frankie had gone too far to be allowed to stay around Ben Spencer's daughter any longer.

Frankie put his hands on her shoulder and pulled her even closer. "I was wrong to drink the whiskey. It does bad things to me. I promise I will not drink it again. I want to make your father proud of me, Mardita. He gave me back my gun, and he is a good man for helping me. I will get a job and make something out of myself. I will work hard, and someday you and your papa will be proud of me. Comprendes, Mardita? Understand?"

As tears came to Mardee's eyes, she threw her arms around him. "Frankie, you've been such a good friend to me always. I will miss you so much."

For several minutes he held the sobbing girl close. Then he tenderly pushed her back. "I must go, querida. But I will come back to see you. Belen is not too far away. I will work hard and try to show your father what I can do. Promise me one thing, mi hita: if you ever need me, let me know, and I will come to help you. You have always been like a little sister to me. Remember how I used to chase the boys away who teased you at school? I have always loved you, and I always will. Siempre. Understand, mi hita, always. Now stop the rain coming down."

Frankie softly rubbed one tearstained cheek with his large rough hand while Mardee brushed the other with the back of her hand. Looking up into his dark concerned eyes, Mardee demanded with some of her old spirit, "Why does everyone that I love leave me? It isn't fair."

"Life isn't fair, Mardita," was the gentle response, "especially for one so beautiful as you. But I will make things better for you one day. I promise." Frankie brushed the tremulous lips lightly and turned to his horse tied a few steps away. He made a quick sign of the cross and was off in one movement. "Adios, querida."

Mardee watched as the rider vanished in the trees. "Vaya con Dios," she whispered "Go with God, my friend. How can I get along without you, Frankie?"

Frankie had taken care of her from the first day she started school. He had sensed her insecurity at being among the older students in the one-room school. He was four years older and often sat beside her and helped with her scholastic chores. School had been hard for her at first, and the teacher was not as patient with her as her grandmother. But Frankie had always been there with his easy way to quiet her fears and show her how she really could do her reading and sums.

Frankie had also become Sadie's helper when she took over the school. For a while the classroom had been filled to capacity as news of the new teacher spread. Young men, older than Sadie, came to sit on the hard benches and try to learn the lessons in "readin' and writin' and 'rithmetic," as well as to stare at the comely teacher. Frankie helped the overburdened teacher with the younger students, but Mardee always knew she was his favorite. She had but to raise her hand, and he was at her side, making things right, whether it was a word she could not figure out or an unwanted spider that ventured up her desk.

Sadie had immediately recognized Frankie's special qualities. She was amazed at his quickness of mind, as well as his desire for knowledge. He enjoyed being her aide, and she often thought what a wonderful teacher he would make, but she feared there would be no opportunity for higher learning for the boy.

His parents scratched a bare living from a few acres of mountain land, and his father worked only occasionally at the mill for extra money. He immediately spent the silver dollars he was paid at the mill commissary on groceries. He didn't dare take money home because his Mexican wife would spend it on liquor. The dark laughing girl he had married had turned into a brooding unhappy woman as the hard years went by, and the only time she smiled was when she was able to drown her existence in alcohol.

Frankie had finished his education at the rock schoolhouse, and Sadie tried to influence him to go to Santa Fe to St. John's Academy. She had even promised to help him financially, but it was too big a step for the mountain boy. He didn't have the confidence to leave home, so he did the chores and took care of the few head of cattle his father owned. He also tried to keep an eye on his mother so she wouldn't slip off to the bar in Punta and get herself a bottle, because even with no money, she still managed to get her drinks one way or another.

Meanwhile, Frankie came to school occasionally and still helped out. Mardee had always looked forward to his visits.

Sadie had watched the two young people with sad knowing eyes. She knew the sensitive boy cared for the appealing child with a lasting love, but she also knew there was no hope of the relationship maturing. Ben Spencer would have liked Frankie had he known him the way Sadie did, but she knew he would never approve of his daughter's marrying him. The young man had Mexican blood in his veins, and although Ben had many Spanish friends whom he held in high regard, he had often said after a particularly trying time with one of his Mexican laborers, "The Lord didn't have much to do the day he created a Mexican." Sadie shuddered when she heard this remark which she considered sacrilegious, both to the Mexicans and to God.

As Ben Spencer's daughter turned and slowly walked back to the house after Frankie rode out of her life, she shook her head in disbelief when she looked bleakly up into the cloudless sky. "This day is only half gone, and I have said goodbye to two very special people in my life. Dear Lord, what am I going to do?"

7

Roy, John, and Mardee placed their containers of algerita berries, picked that afternoon on a rocky slope about a mile from the house, on the kitchen table. The boys then heaved sighs of relief and quickly headed outdoors to do something more to their liking before their mother figured out more chores.

The short mountain summer was almost over, and Sadie was diligently working on canning and preserving food for winter. The potatoes, carrots, and turnips were dug from the garden and put in soft soil beds in the root cellar to be retrieved in cold weather for soups and stews. She also had many shelves of canned beans, peas, tomatoes, and corn ready for dinner vegetables. Apples, plums, and apricots from the orchard were canned in glass jars for pies and desserts through the year. Raspberries, currents, chokecherries, and algerita berries were now being picked to become jellies and jams. The pumpkins that had been rolled into the cellar would be cut up later and made into the family's favorite pie during the long cold months.

This was a busy time, and everyone helped. Mardee and the younger children worked in the daytime, and Ben and the older boys picked and peeled vegetables and fruit in the evenings. As the jars filled up and the cellar became crowded with produce, Sadie smiled more often and acted a little more lighthearted. Ben would make a trip to Mountainair in October and buy flour, sugar, salt, coffee, oatmeal, macaroni, and other miscellaneous supplies, and the family would be set for winter.

This was a social time of the year as well. Neighbors helped each other harvest hay and beans. Dinner tables piled high with the culinary specialties of each farm wife made the hard work enjoyable. When a beef or a hog was butchered, neighbors were invited for music and dancing and food. Just the smell of fresh pork ribs was enough motivation for neighbors to come miles through the pinon-scented hills. The meat that wasn't used for community celebrations would be canned and smoked and dried for the winter months.

Mardee was looking forward to a harvest square dance that would be held in her father's commissary this coming Saturday night. This was the first social event in the community since the statehood celebration, and Mardee was ready to dance and laugh again. But Jeff wouldn't be here to dance with. Her father had gotten only one short note from him since he had gone to Santa Fe, and he said he was very busy with his new job. But Mardee's exuberant young optimism was unclouded at the prospect of dancing only with neighborhood boys. She loved to square dance with anyone, and perhaps someone interesting would drift in.

Sadie and Mardee were cleaning the berries when a sudden noise penetrated the silence of the kitchen. "Ooga-ooga!" split the cool mountain air.

"What in Heaven's name?" Sadie asked as she rushed to the kitchen door with Mardee right behind her. They couldn't believe their eyes at the sight that was parked in their yard. Ben sat smiling inside the contraption in a swirl of dust as his merry eyes spotted his astounded women.

"Benjamin Boyd Spencer, what have you done now?" Sadie demanded.

Ben opened the door and stepped out of his new Model T Ford he had just purchased from the Griffin Motor Company in Mountainair. Fanning the dust from his face, he approached Sadie and Mardee with a proud swagger. "I bought this car for us, Sadie. You know, we must have some way to get around since Mardee burned up our buggy." Ben then turned slowly back to his prize and circled it, kicking the hard little tires. He stopped at the hood and lifted it, gazing in at the clean new motor admiringly. "Come here, boys, and let me show you a mighty pretty piece of machinery."

Roy walked over with his brother as he cast a guilty look toward Mardee. They had a secret, and the secret was that Roy was really the culprit who had burned up the family buggy. While Mardee was busy washing one Monday morning with her washpot boiling over a brisk fire, Roy had slipped into the buggy with some Prince Albert tobacco and was trying his hand at smoking like his big brothers. He held the tobacco in one hand and a cigarette paper in the other and tried to roll a cigarette the way he had seen men do it, but he found it more complicated than he had imagined. It was hard to hold a delicate paper in one hand and pour tobacco in it with the other, and he awkwardly spilled tobacco all over the buggy seat.

Finally, by putting the paper on the seat and using both hands to pour the tobacco and then to roll the cigarette, he had succeeded in getting some semblance of the prize he sought. He then struck several matches in an attempt to get the cigarette lighted. When he finally got it lit and was drawing the acrid smoke into his lungs, he suddenly had a coughing fit. But he was determined and was finally able to take several deep puffs. However, he was suddenly feeling very dizzy and nauseated. He hastily evacuated the buggy, knowing he would be in big trouble if he dirtied his father's buggy.

He fell headfirst on the ground and lay there as the world spun crazily. It was several minutes before he had the strength to crawl to the house, up the stairs and onto his bed where he lay for an hour feeling deathly ill. He silently swore he would never touch tobacco again if God would let him live.

When Roy finally got up he walked over to his window and looked down into the back yard where Mardee was hanging out white sheets on the clothesline. Then his eyes fastened on the far side of the yard where the buggy sat in the shade of a big juniper tree. He still felt weak, and his legs nearly went out from under him when he saw the smoke. He instantly realized he had left the lighted cigarette on the seat.

As Roy ran down the stairs he heard Mardee calling, "Roy, Roy, bring some water! We've got a fire!"

Roy grabbed the water bucket out of the kitchen and joined Mardee, who was throwing her rinse water on the flames. The two worked frantically trying to squelch the fire, but it was to no avail. The snappy buggy that Ben Spencer had driven with the matched bay horses was beyond help. The wooden body covered with fancy leather was gone in no time, and all that remained was the axle and the wheel hubs.

Roy had been white with fear, sickness, and shame as he and Mardee viewed the smoking remains. He knew he had done a very bad thing, and he also knew he would be in deep trouble with his father.

Mardee had looked down at her brother, and her heart melted. She knew from his white face and sick eyes what the little boy had done. "Were you smoking in there, Roy?" she asked softly.

Tears had welled up in his sad blue eyes, and Roy nodded his head. "I'm sorry," he gulped. "Mardee, what am I going to do? Papa will beat me."

"No, he won't," Mardee had said quickly. "You know, Roy, I had a very big fire under my washpot. One of the sparks could have blown into the buggy."

Roy had looked up at his big sister with a glint of hope. "Do you think that happened, Mardee?"

"I'm sure that happened," Mardee had announced firmly. "Don't worry about it. It was an accident. Papa won't beat me." She smiled reassuringly at her upset little brother and held him close. "You don't feel very well. Let's get you in the house and give you some tea to settle your stomach."

Anyway, Ben had been thinking about buying one of those new inventions called a "car" that Henry Ford had built. Now he had the impetus he needed, and best of all, Sadie couldn't object. The next week he headed to town where Howard Griffin sold him a new Model T Ford for $400, and he also threw in a driving lesson.

In no time Ben and his boys had completed their inspection of the new car, and Ben announced, "Hop in, everyone. We're going for a ride!"

Sadie caught her breath and gasped. "Mr. Spencer, I will not get in that contraption."

But Ben lifted her bodily and put her on the front seat as Roy and John and Mardee piled happily into the back. Roy snuggled into the curve of Mardee's arm as he looked up into her eyes with a message only for the two of them. She squeezed him and whispered, "You see, everything is all right; in fact, it's wonderful!"

Ben then went to the front of the car and gave the crank several brisk turns. The motor burst into life, and the whole car vibrated as the passengers shuddered at the noise.

Ben leaped into the car and playfully patted Sadie's knee. "Remember this day forever, Sadie. The first time you rode in a car!"

"I'm sure I will," Sadie whispered weakly.

The car moved forward with a jerk as John banged his head into the door on his side. Sadie slid over against Ben, and Mardee held tightly to Roy. Sadie quickly righted herself and started praying.

"We'll drive over to the mill and pick up the other boys," Ben said over the roar of the engine.

The car bounced over the rough rutted road as the passengers in the back seat laughed and shouted hysterically. Sadie clutched her hair as if it were going to blow away. Ben glanced sideways nervously as he realized she knew he didn't know how to drive this machine very well. She thinks the end of the world has come, he told himself amusedly, and his confidence increased.

As they approached the turn-off to the mill, Ben twisted the steering wheel sharply to the left and forgot to apply the brake. He had turned too abruptly, and there was a bruising jolt as the front wheel hit the unyielding side of the ditch, and the car coughed and died. The passengers sat in shocked silence as the car leaned at an uncomfortable angle in the ditch.

Sadie found her voice. "Mr. Spencer," she shrilled . "Get me out of this monster. You are going to kill us all. Get these children out immediately. Do you hear me?"

Ben sat quietly for a few moments and then turned slowly and painfully to his wife. "Get control of yourself, woman," he said roughly. "Are you all right, children?"

"We're fine," Roy and John chorused. With Mardee holding on to them, they were fearless.

By now Sadie had scrambled over the tilting seat and was pushing her door open. "I'm getting out of here," she said, not waiting for her husband to help her. She almost fell to the ground, but immediately picked herself up.

"Come on, children, we are going to walk home."

Roy and John clambered out their back door, but Mardee stayed put. "I'll help Papa."

"Suit yourself," Sadie sniffed as she gathered up her little boys and headed back down the road.

Actually, Ben had almost had the breath knocked out of him by the steering wheel, but he was breathing better now. He looked back at his irate wife marching down the road and chuckled, "She's as mad as an old wet hen." Turning to Mardee, he said, "I'll go get some of the men to help me push this thing out of the ditch, and we'll finish our ride. How's that sound, Mardeebird?"

"Wonderful," she giggled. "Teach me how to drive this car, Papa. I know you'll teach Floyd. I want to learn, too. Please, Papa, please!"

Ben smiled at his daughter. "Too bad you can't make the damned thing stop when you say whoa!"

8

The August Saturday morning dawned bright and beautiful. Mardee rose early and helped Sadie with the chores.

Sadie was complaining of palpitations of the heart after yesterday's automobile fiasco, so Mardee's strong quick hands made short work of the morning routine as she deftly washed dishes, swept, cleaned, and gathered eggs. Mardee was concerned for her stepmother.

Sadie had always complained about her heart when she was stressed, and her father had assured her it was only nerves. But in the back of Mardee's mind, the picture of her grandmother whose heart had stopped beating was still a hurtful and anxious memory.

Mardee was starting to appreciate and understand this woman. She was beginning to realize that her cold and uncaring exterior really masked a vulnerable and unsure personality. Her quiet years on a Kansas farm had not prepared her for life on the New Mexico frontier with bombastic Ben Spencer for a husband. She craved a more peaceful spiritual existence. The times when she could retire to her bedroom and lose herself in her Bible provided spiritual inspiration to her soul. The realities of a harsh life and a demanding husband were softened as she read and rejoiced in God's promises.

Mardee now realized that Mother Spencer felt compassion for her and her youthful frustrations. When Mardee had moped around with a sad and martyred face after Jeff Corbin had gone to Santa Fe, she had come in from a solitary walk one afternoon to find a luscious lemon pie sitting on the kitchen table. She'd had little appetite in the dark days after Jeff left, but the sight of that beautiful golden brown mound of meringue did wonders for her empty stomach.

"Mardee, I baked your favorite pie. Do you want a piece now?"

Mardee looked with disbelief from the pie to her stepmother.

"It's just for you, Mardee," Sadie continued matter-of-factly.

Sadie then cut Mardee a generous slice and got her a cool glass of water from the water bucket. Mardee sat down to her treat as the depressed feelings she had been struggling with started to lighten.

"Please take some, too, Mother Spencer," she said shyly.

"Thank you, I will," Sadie said, her face breaking into a smile. "I hope it is good."

"It is wonderful!" Mardee pronounced. "And you baked it just for me?" she asked incredulously.

Sadie finished cutting her small slice and sat down carefully and picked up her fork before she answered. "Mardee, one would think I have never done anything for you before. I do many things for you every day." She looked at Mardee with the usual disapproval.

"I know," Mardee hastened to explain. "But nothing so special as one of your lemon pies."

Sadie's tight face smoothed into tenderness. "Well, perhaps I should do it more often." Sadie cleared her throat and lowered her head, slightly embarrassed.

Sadie then took a bite of pie and raised her head resolutely. "Mardee, I know you have been going through a bad time. I also know you don't think I know or care what happens to you. But I do understand, and I do care. You know, Mardee, I have four boys, but do I have any daughters?" She paused and looked straight at Mardee. "Yes," she continued, "I have you. Please remember this when you have problems."

Mardee stared at her stepmother wide-eyed. Then her loving nature erupted and she dropped her fork, ran around the table, and knelt by Sadie, throwing her arms around her waist and laying her head in her lap. Tears ran down her cheeks as the thin stiff hand of her stepmother awkwardly patted her hair. "It's all right, child," came the soft words.

She does like me, were the words that repeated themselves over and over in Mardee's head.

Sadie gave her a hankie to wipe her damp face, and Mardee dabbed at the wet spot on her stepmother's dress. "Don't worry, Mardee," Sadie reassured her. "Tears dry fast, especially yours." She smiled at the disheveled girl and helped her stand. "Finish your pie before the boys come in and finish it for you."

Mardee returned to her seat, and with a feeling of new found closeness for her stepmother, asked, "Mother Spencer, did you ever love anyone when you were my age?"

This unexpected question caused Sadie's fork to pause in midair. Her striking blue eyes softened, and she replied, "Oh yes, my dear. I loved a young man who came to work on our farm in Kansas, and I wanted to marry him."

Mardee could hardly contain herself at this unexpected information. "What happened?" she asked quickly.

"My father didn't approve. I was too young, he thought." Sadie suddenly got up, taking her unfinished pie with her. Mardee saw the glint of tears in her eyes.

Mardee finished her pie in silence as Sadie busied herself around the kitchen. She does know, she told herself. Mother Spencer does know what it means to love someone.

"Thank you so much for the pie, Mother Spencer," Mardee said. "And thank you for understanding. I love you."

Mardee's thoughts returned to the present as Ben banged in the door shouting directives. "Fix us a sandwich, Sadie. Floyd and Mardee and I are going for a driving lesson."

Mardee jumped up to help her stepmother. This was going to be an extra special day. She would learn to drive that car, and she wouldn't drive it into a ditch! Then there was the square dance tonight. Life is so wonderful! she thought as she and Sadie exchanged smiles.

9

After everyone had gone, Sadie worked on her berries, picking stems and overripe ones out of the batch and placing the good ones in a large pot, just covering them with water.

Following her time-tested recipe closely, in two hours the clear red jelly told her before she tasted it that it was just right. Sadie prided herself on her perfect jellies.

Sometimes Sadie made jam out of raspberries, plums, or apricots. She used the same recipe for jam as for jelly; it just took a little longer to make, but it was a good change in the cold winter months.

Sadie was diligently cleaning up after her jelly project when she heard a car drive up. She was surprised that the driving lesson was over so soon. She didn't look up from her work until she heard a knock and was surprised to see a man at the kitchen door, and it wasn't Ben. Wiping her hands on her apron, she opened the door.

The large Spanish man with a big pistol on his hip took off his hat and bowed slightly, saying, "Mrs. Spencer, I am Alfredo Chavez, the deputy sheriff from Belen. I need to talk to Mr. Spencer."

"I'm afraid he isn't here, sir," Sadie said frowning. "Can I help you?"

The deputy looked self-consciously at his hat as he twisted it in his hands. After a moment's hesitation he replied, "Maybe you can. I have a tip that a man I have a warrant for is hiding near here in a rock house. Do you happen to know where that house is?"

"Yes, I do," she answered slowly, "but I can't leave my work right now to show you." Sadie knew the house was about a mile and a half away.

"Is there anyone else around who could show me?" the deputy sheriff asked anxiously. "I have come all the way from Belen."

Just then John and Roy, who had been playing a short distance from the house, came running up to see who the visitor was. "Actually, the boys could show you where this place is," Sadie said. "But don't you let them go up to the house with you."

The deputy's face brightened. "That would help me very much, Mrs. Spencer. I promise I will keep the boys out of danger."

"All right," Sadie said, looking thoughtful. "You can see the house a quarter of a mile before you get to it. Let the boys out of the car there, and they can walk back." Turning to John and Roy she said, "Go with Deputy Chavez, boys. Point out the old rock house down the road. He needs to check it."

The boys got delightedly into his car. They felt very grown up to be riding alone with the deputy on this special mission.

The lawman bumped down the mountain road with his guides, and it wasn't long before the boys pointed out the rock house situated in a clearing a short distance from the road. Deputy Chavez took a rifle from the back seat of his car and opened the door. "You boys go on back home now," he instructed. "Thanks for the help. Muchas gracias."

The lawman never once looked back, or he would have seen the boys creeping along behind him. This was too big an adventure for them to miss.

As he approached the house, Chavez paused behind a bush to look around. The house was rundown and apparently vacant. The front door swung open partway, and a window in the attic was just a gaping hole with no glass.

Suddenly the deputy spotted the boys. He was aggravated at first, but then he had an idea. "John," he whispered, "you slip through the door to see if anyone is in there. I'll be out here with my gun covering you."

John was eager to help the deputy, but as Roy started to follow him Chavez grabbed his sleeve and shook his head, to Roy's disappointment.

John carefully approached the door, turned sideways, and disappeared. Simultaneously, there was a loud noise and movement at the attic window. Chavez stepped back to raise his gun, but he caught his heel on a rock and fell backwards as his gun discharged.

When John hurriedly emerged from the door, Roy was crouched in fear with his hands over his ears, the deputy sheriff sat on his backside holding his rifle at an upward angle, and a skinny black cat was catapulting through the trees.

"Lord have mercy," John yelled, "it was only a black cat. What are you shooting at?"

Deputy Chavez pulled himself to his feet. "S-s-sorry, boys," he stuttered. "I thought my suspect was jumping out the window."

The boys returned home with mixed feelings of pride and disappointment after saying goodbye to Deputy Chavez. After all, they hadn't captured anything, not even the cat, so they went about finishing their game of mumblepeg with their pocket knives just as if nothing had happened.

When Ben and Floyd and Mardee finally drove up, John and Roy ran to their father, telling him about their adventure. When they finished Ben said in wonderment, "So Chavez sent you in to flush a man out, and then he fell on his fat ass?"

"That's right, Papa," John replied, nodding vigorously and beaming at his own importance.

Ben threw back his head and laughed. Then turning to go in the house, he mumbled, "It's a good thing the son-of-a-bitch didn't shoot one of my boys." Putting a hand on each son's shoulder, he said jovially, "Good job, boys. Let's go eat. Just don't tell your mother what happened."

A few hours later the bungling deputy from Belen was forgotten as everyone gathered for the square dance. Large families came in wagons, small families came in buggies, and single people came by horseback. The musicians went about the business of tuning their instruments as people caught up with their visiting. The children ran shouting and laughing and playing games that would last until it got too dark for them to see. They would then curl up on pallets in the corner of the commisary dance floor and go to sleep.

Shortly, the fiddlers began a fast square dance piece, and Ben motioned for the dancing to begin. Freshly shaven men in clean worn pants and shirts led their full-skirted women onto the floor and twirled them around and around.

Swing your partner and do, ce, do,
All around the ring you go,
Meet your partner at the end,
And take that pretty girl home again.

After Ben finished calling the first number he walked over and grabbed the broom. "Broom Dance," he announced to the noisy crowd. "When I call 'change partners,' I'll grab one of your lovely women and the man left without a partner has to dance with this broom."

The crowd loved this dance. Ben waited until a pretty farm wife danced by, then quickly called for the change of partners as he took his prize. Chaos reigned while everyone searched wildly for a partner. Kurt Mason, who had joined the dancers for a while as Old Pike took over the fiddle, was the unlucky one left standing in the middle of the floor. "Here, Kurt," Ben said in mock sympathy as he thrust the broom at him. "Matilda wants to dance with you!"

Kurt reluctantly moved awkwardly around with the broom, self-conscious and red-faced. The grace with which he wielded the magic fiddle bow didn't extend to his long legs. But as Mardee came swirling by, he quickly reached for her and yelled, "Change partners!" Handing the broom to the luckless man now standing in the middle of the room with a surprised look on his face, he deftly led Mardee toward the door of the commissary.

"I've got to get out in the fresh air where I can breathe," he explained as he led her away from the building. "You'll be dancing all night, Mardee. Take a break so you can rest."

"Sure," Mardee said as she looked up into the tall musician's face. "But I really never get tired of dancing."

Kurt knew this, of course. He had watched her many times as he played the fiddle. She danced every dance with the beauty and exuberance of a young deer. She always followed her partner perfectly, whether it was a young boy who didn't really know how to dance or an old man who had lost his dancing skills. Her smiling face and infectious laugh made each partner feel special for the short time she danced with him.

Kurt had decided to put his fiddle down tonight and claim a dance from this tantalizing girl. He was a simple boy who asked nothing more than to play music, but he was beginning to notice that Mardee was a beautiful song, herself.

"You're a very good dancer, Mardee," Kurt said shyly. "Do you like my music?" The country boy gazed at Mardee adoringly.

"I love your music, Kurt," Mardee answered softly. Putting her hands up on his chest, she smiled up into his serious face. "Would you write me a song? A song called *The Manzano Hummingbird?*"

"What's a hummingbird, Mardee?" Kurt asked as he gazed dreamily down into her upturned face.

"A brightly colored little bird that whirs through the air looking for honey, just like me," Mardee answered, repeating her grandmother's description.

Kurt was a little confused as he realized the conversation wasn't going where he had hoped it would. "I never wrote that kind of a song," he muttered.

"Oh, you can." Mardee said, staring up into his dazed face. "You are so talented you can do anything. Don't I inspire you just a little bit so you can write a song for me?" She turned her head at an angle and looked up at him appealingly. "Promise me you'll do it, Kurt."

Suddenly Mardee felt a hand on her shoulder. "Promise her anything, Kurt. A girl as beautiful as this one should have anything she wants."

Mardee whirled to discover a man dressed all in black, a big black hat on his head. As she searched the darkness for a face, a hearty laugh filled the dark night air. "So soon, Mardita, you don't remember me? I leave only a short time and come back to find you with Kurt." Extending a hand to Kurt, he said, "Como estas, amigo. Good to see you again."

Mardee stood dumbfounded as the men shook hands. There was a big difference in Frankie. His voice was more assured, his movements more confident. He was not the mountain boy any longer; he was now a man.

She threw herself at him and scolded, "How can I know you in the dark dressed all in black? And you are so tall!" She stepped back to look up at him with wondering eyes.

"And you are so little with your red hair and your starry eyes, but I know you, little one." Frankie put his arm around her waist and pulled her to him. "I missed you, Mardita," he whispered in her ear.

Mardee snuggled into the curve of his arm, feeling safer and happier than she had in a long time. "Oh Frankie, it is so good to see you! I missed you, too."

"I'd better get back to the music," Kurt said to the air. He knew they were lost in their own world.

Frankie looked tenderly down into Mardee's flushed face and pushed his hat back to kiss her on the forehead. But just then he saw the outline of Ben Spencer coming out the door. Pushing Mardee gently back, he whispered, "Your papa is coming. I want to talk to him. You go back in to the baile. I will come and dance with you soon."

Mardee hurried past her father as Frankie stuck out his hand. "Hello, Mr. Spencer. I was coming to talk to you."

"Hello, Frankie," Ben replied guardedly. "How are you doing?"

"Muy bien," Frankie answered. "I am to receive a promotion soon. I want to thank you very much for helping me get this good job. I know they give me the job because of you. They know you are a good man, and I am working very hard to show them I am a good man, too. I do not want to disappoint you, or them, sir."

Ben found himself hesitating. He had meant to tell Frankie to stay away from his daughter, but after these gracious words it seemed difficult. "That is good news, Frankie. Mrs. Spencer always had confidence in you, so I'm glad to hear she is right."

"She is a wonderful woman, Senora Spencer. She taught me so much in school that is helping me now. She is an angel. I would like to thank her. Is she here?" Frankie asked warmly.

"No," Ben said hastily, "she has probably retired at home. But I will give her your kind words." Ben looked Frankie over more closely now that his eyes had grown accustomed to the darkness. He stood before the older man squarely, his eyes steady as he returned Ben's straight gaze. Ben detected new strength in the man since he had last seen him.

Frankie then reached in his shirt pocket and brought out a roll of money. Extending it, he said, "Mr. Spencer, I will not be going on to Punta tonight. Would you please give this money to my father? My mother is sick, and he needs money to take her to the doctor in Albuquerque."

"Of course, Frankie, I will see that your father gets this money," Ben replied, putting it in his pocket.

"Thank you so much, sir. Now if you will excuse me, I would like to go inside."

Ben watched as Frankie walked off with light quick steps, thinking to himself that this dance wasn't turning out to be such a good one for him. First Mardee had disappeared into the darkness with the fiddler. Then he had found her in the arms of the half-breed who wasn't going to be easy to chase off anymore.

Hell, I sent him to Belen to get rid of him, he thought impatiently, not to have him come back thinking he's a hero. Ben sighed to himself as he realized the dances were no longer the simple good times he had always enjoyed in the past. His young daughter was definitely complicating his life.

10

After Ben returned to the commissary he edged over to the corner where the children were resting on pallets on the floor. Old Lou Tompkins' daughter, Lola, was watching over them. Their parents would dance until dawn, then be treated to breakfast, and then gather up the sleeping children and head for home.

Ben noted that Lola was developing into an attractive young woman. This was the first time Old Lou had let her attend a dance, and he had only brought her to take care of the younger children.

"Thank you for watching the children, Lola," Ben said to the girl. "You are doing a good job."

Lola looked up shyly from under her dark bangs. She had seldom been off the farm and didn't know how to properly address adults, but she smiled and her dark eyes sparkled. She doesn't know what to say, but her eyes do it for her, Ben thought.

Just then Old Lou sauntered over. "That thar's my gal, Ben, and she's a good little thing. She air smart, too. She done right good in school with Miz Spencer, but I been keepin' her home to work lately."

"I can see she is a good worker, Lou," Ben replied slowly. "And she's a mighty pretty young thing. Since she's done such a good job here tonight, how about it if I find her a partner to dance a while? I'm going to call some square dances now, and I'll call some easy ones she won't have any trouble with. You can keep an eye on the young'uns for a while, can't you?"

Old Lou looked uncertain. He was proud of his pretty daughter, and he didn't want her taking a shine to a young fellow and marrying too soon. But he wanted to stay in good with his friend, and besides, he had a favor to ask of Ben, so he nodded his approval.

Ben took Lola by the hand and led her over to Floyd, who lounged against the wall. "Dance with her, son," he smilingly ordered. "This is Lola, you know."

"Sure, Papa," Floyd said with a smile as he escorted her onto the dance floor. A lively schottische was being played, and Lola's shy beauty was instantly transformed into life as she executed the steps easily. Floyd had his father's love for dancing, and he was pleased to display his attractive new partner.

"Good job, Lola," Mardee said breathlessly as she and Frankie whirled past. Although Lola was younger than Mardee, they had been friends in school, and Mardee had missed her after she had finished school. She's growing up, Mardee realized.

But Mardee's thoughts about the younger girl were quickly erased as she danced with Frankie. She knew how much more fun the dance had become as she followed the lead of her handsome partner. He had the innate love of music and dancing from his mother's people. His tall dark good looks enhanced the perfection of her girlish beauty, and the pairing of the two produced an intoxicating image.

Mardee loved the feel of her partner's rhythmic muscled body, and his laughing eyes were hypnotic. Frankie had always been her friend, but she was beginning to have a strange new feeling. Something is different about him, she thought.

The music soon settled down into the slower strains of *Cielito Lindo*. Frankie sang the words softly in Mardee's ear as he held her close. "Ay, ay, ay, ay, canta y no llores; porque cantando se allegran Cielito Lindo los corazones." Then he whispered, "Always sing, mi hita, and don't cry. Because you are always in my heart. Si, siempre en mi corazon."

As the romantic song ended Frankie led Mardee outside, and under a pungent pinon tree he took her in his arms. All those years of thwarted love poured from his demanding lips to her soft yielding mouth. "I have loved you always," he whispered. You know that, mi hita?"

Mardee couldn't speak as she tried to understand her new feelings. But Frankie pulled her closer. "Even when you were a little girl, I loved you. I will never love anyone else. Say you feel something for me, querida."

But I love Jeff, Mardee thought. Frankie is just my good friend. But I did enjoy his kisses. She felt confused as she looked up at him, and finally replied, "Frankie I have always loved you, as a friend."

Frankie put his hand under her chin and kissed her nose. "You didn't kiss me as a friend, little one." And then with a frown on his face, he asked, "Are you thinking of the judge?"

Mardee dropped her eyes.

"Yes, you are thinking of el juez, Jeff Corbin," Frankie said as he looked sadly into her eyes. "He will only hurt you, querida. He loves his job more than he loves you."

Mardee drew back, stamping her foot. "He does love me. I think I know more than you do about how he feels."

"No importa," Frankie said as he took her arm with a grin. "Let's go back to dance. Your father will come looking for you."

Ben had been watching for Mardee and Frankie to return, and when he saw them come in he finished his square dance and turned the music back to Kurt. He eased back over to where Lou Tompkins was minding the sleepy children.

Old Lou had his eagle eye on his own daughter who was having more fun than she had ever dreamed possible. "I need to talk to you, Ben," he said slowly, chewing his tobacco as he spoke. "It's about Lola."

"What about Lola?"

"Wal, she finished eighth grade this year, and I don't see no need o' sending her to school no more. She needs to stay home and help with the work and the young'uns. She cooks beans and tortillas fine, but I was a wonderin' if maybe she could come to yore house for a while and learn how to cook white folks' food, like biscuits and rolls and pies and cakes. My Indian wife don't know how to teach her to do much around a house, either. Now Sadie could make a lady out o' her and teach her to clean house and wash and cook. Then if that wife o' mine gets mad and leaves, I'll have me someone to take care o' me. So how about it?

Ben knew Lola was the one child Old Lou loved with all his hard heart. She was not the Indian woman's child, and he knew she was not treated well by her stepmother. In Old Lou's mind it was perfectly all right if he decided to beat his children, but he didn't want his wife beating Lola. He wanted her under Sadie's influence for her own good as well as his own satisfaction.

"How does Lola feel about this, Lou?" Ben asked.

"It's no matter, Ben," Lou replied. "I be the boss o' that child. She goes whar I tells her to go."

"Of course, Lou, I understand that," Ben said softly. "Let me talk to Sadie, and I'll let you know."

A rare smile broke the old man's craggy features. "Thanks, Ben. I'm beholden to you." Then the smile quickly vanished. "I'll tell her to work hard, or I'll break ever' bone in her body."

The music suddenly claimed Ben's attention as Kurt Mason's melodious voice filled the room. Kurt seldom sang, since he preferred to play his fiddle, but he had a pleasing baritone voice when he wanted to use it. His cousin picked an accompaniment on the guitar as he sang a song Ben had never heard before:

She has eyes as bright as the morning star,
And lips the color of the red, red rose,
She's the very first girl that I ever loved,
And my love for her will always grow.
My pretty Manzano hummingbird,
Don't you know that I love you?
I hope someday you'll fly my way
And make all my dreams come true.

Kurt then put his fiddle to his shoulder and played the soft mournful melody through before he sang the chorus:

My pretty Manzano hummingbird,
Do not fly into the redhot fire,
As you sing and fly and search afar
For the bittersweet honey your heart desires.
My pretty Manzano hummingbird,
Do not fly into the redhot fire.

When Kurt finished, he pointed his fiddle bow at Mardee and bowed. Everyone laughed and stared over at the recipient of the song and then clapped at her red-faced embarrassment. Kurt hadn't gotten the girl that night, but he knew she would never forget him now.

When Mardee crawled into bed in the wee hours of the morning, she went to sleep to the strains of Kurt's song still playing in her head and the sweetness of Frankie's kisses still lingering on her lips.

"What a wonderful night," she murmured as she stretched out luxuriously in her feather bed.

11

Lola had now come to live with the family and was helping with the chores. Sadie found her an apt student who learned eagerly and worked with a smile. She had quickly forgotten her shyness and had become one of the family. In a short time she had worked her way past Sadie's cold exterior and entrenched her endearing personality into everyone's hearts. Sadie had taught her in school, so she already had a genuine fondness for the girl. The boys found her an interesting and attractive creature, and they included her in their conversations and activities.

Ben appreciated Lola's gratitude at being allowed to stay with them, and noted with approval her industrious manner. Mardee, never having had a sister, enjoyed this new relationship. The girls talked and giggled and shared their innermost thoughts.

One day Sadie and Lola were preparing apple butter when Mardee burst in, having just returned from delivering her father's lunch. She waved a letter excitedly in Sadie's face. "Papa got a letter from Jeff today. He has a job for me if I can go to Santa Fe."

"Control yourself, girl," Sadie admonished. "I'm in the middle of these apples, and I don't have time to read any letters right now. Your father and I will discuss it tonight. Now get a paring knife and help Lola peel that basket of apples."

"Yes ma'am," Mardee replied. She winked at Lola, and the younger girl's eyes sparkled as she returned the wink. Mardee had told her all about Jeff, and she could hardly wait to hear what was in the letter.

The prospect of going to Santa Fe to work was almost beyond Mardee's imagination, and the thought of seeing Jeff again gave her a weak feeling and a pounding heart all at the same time. In the two months since he had gone, her heart and body ached every day for the look and touch of him. Her knife whirred around the apples as she silently prayed to be allowed to go.

"Careful, Mardee, you're going to cut your finger," Sadie sternly warned. "We don't need blood in the apple butter."

Mardee lifted appealing eyes to her stepmother. "Oh Mother Spencer, please let me go."

But before she could get an answer there was a sharp knock at the door. Mardee rose swiftly and ran to the door, pushing the screen open. "Hello, mi hita," Frankie Moseby said softly to the amazed girl.

"What are you doing here, Frankie?" she asked, forgetting her manners.

Seeing Sadie hovering in the background, he pushed past the startled young girl and entered the kitchen. "Mrs. Spencer, my mother has died, and I am on my way to Punta de Agua. I stopped to tell you and Mr. Spencer this sad news. The funeral is tomorrow in the church, and I invite all of you to come." His dark eyes were dry, but his face was drawn in pain and sadness.

Sadie placed her hand on his arm. "I'm so sorry, Frankie." She turned quickly and picked up a loaf of freshly made bread and some rolls from the table and put them into a sack. "I'll add a couple of jars of apple butter. Maybe this will come in handy."

"Thank you, dear Mrs. Spencer. This bread is a delicious treat, and it is very special coming from you." Taking the sack, Frankie turned to leave as Mardee grabbed his hand. They walked out in silence to the sweaty horse tied to a fence post.

"I must go, Mardita. My father needs me," he said as he mounted.

Mardee looked up into the young man's tortured face. "Oh Frankie, I'm so sorry." She grasped his strong hand. "I will try to come to the funeral. I want to be by your side if I can."

Frankie gently retrieved his hand. "I know, dear Mardee." He had never called her by her name before, she couldn't help noticing. "I am so sorry, too. I am so sorry she didn't get to a doctor sooner. I am so sorry she couldn't stay away from the alcoholica. I am so sorry I wasn't a better son."

"It's not your fault," Mardee said firmly. "You have always been a very good son. She loved you dearly and was so proud of you. You were not the reason for her unhappiness. Dear Frankie, don't be so sad. I will be there with you tomorrow, I promise."

"I would like that, mi hita," Frankie said softly. As he rode away, Mardee whispered, "Vaya con Dios, mi amigo. Go with God, and may He give you comfort in your sorrow."

12

The next morning Ben had to take a load of lumber to Belen, so he decided that Mardee would represent the family at the funeral. She could handle the new car easily, and he trusted her to make the drive to Punta. John would go with her.

Floyd and Charlie would go with Ben to help unload the lumber. Sadie didn't approve of Mardee going off in the car, but she couldn't really complain about needing her at home because she had Lola with her now. She made one weak attempt to voice her objections. "Mr. Spencer, Mardee is too young to be going off by herself in that contraption."

Ben dismissed her comment with a wave of his hand."She is eighteen years old now; she's a woman, and a very capable one. She's a good driver, and John will be with her to help with any emergencies."

Little Roy pulled himself up, stuck out his square jaw, and said, "Papa, I want to go. I can help, too."

Mardee put her arm around her little brother. "Let him, Papa. I want him with me so we can have a fun trip before I leave."

The night before Sadie and Ben had finally agreed that Mardee could work part time in Santa Fe and attend school part time.

"The boys can play in the Indian Ruins while I'm at the funeral, and I'll pick them up when the service is over." She smiled down at Roy's eager upturned face and bent down to kiss his forehead.

"All right," Ben relented. "Behave yourselves, boys, or this will be your last trip. Watch for snakes in those ruins."

Mardee and the boys were soon headed down the rutted dirt road that ran east from the foothills. She turned north about three miles away from the town of Mountainair.

Mountainair had sprouted up as the Belen Cutoff Railroad was being built through the Abo Pass in 1903. The town had grown fast since it was the junction between the Santa Fe and the New Mexico Central Railroads. Ben Spencer, who had furnished the timber for the ties when the railroad was built over the mountains, became the vice president and treasurer of the Abo Land Company that surveyed 120 acres for the original townsite of Mountainair. A post office was also established in 1903, and the mail was carried by horseback from Albuquerque to Eastview and then on to Mountainair until the trains began to run.

The railroads offered special fares to Mountainair to encourage people to come to the annual Chatauqua festivities. They hoped some of the people would decide to homestead the fertile farm and ranch land. Mountainair soon became a thriving little western town, and the Spencer family always looked forward to their visits there to buy supplies.

Ben was paid for his services to the Abo Land Company with four choice lots in the new town. He built two buildings on the lots and Sadie hoped to live there some day and get away from the mountain ranch, but for now, Ben used one of the buildings for a hardware store and the other as a residence for his lumber yard manager.

Meanwhile, the boys noticed that they weren't on the regular road to Mountainair anymore. "Where are we going, Mardee?" Roy asked. "Aren't we going through Mountainair?"

"Not today, little brother," Mardee replied, tousling his blonde curls affectionately. "We don't have to. The funeral is in Punta de Agua."

"What's Punta de Agua?" John asked quickly.

"It's a town, silly," Mardee laughingly answered. "It means water point in English. There's a spring there. That's why the Tigua Indians chose to live there. They could farm there, and with the deer they killed, they had plenty of food. I'll just give you a little New Mexico history now, boys."

She smiled over at her brothers. "When Juan de Onate, a Spanish Conquistador, came to this country in 1598, many years ago, he found 600 Tigua Indians living there. A few years later some Franciscan friars from Spain established a mission and built the magnificent Mission Church of the Immaculate Conception. You will see the ruins of that church today, as well as the rooms where the priests and their helpers lived."

"Are Indians still living there today?" Roy asked, his blue eyes alive with interest.

"No," Mardee answered. "No one really knows why they left their mission, but it may be because there was a drought and the water dried up, or maybe they all got sick from a bad sickness, but it was probably because the Apache Indians from the west attacked, killing them and raiding their food. Or maybe they moved to the Isleta Indian Pueblo on the Rio Grande over toward Albuquerque. Anyway, they were very ancient people who lived there, and brave Spanish priests came to teach them about God. The Indians had never heard about our God."

It was difficult for the boys to understand people who had never been told about God because their mother had spoken of God to them since they could remember. "Did they like to hear about God?" John asked after a pause.

Mardee laughed. "They were probably very much like us. Some of us want to hear about God more than others do." She smiled and added, "It's too bad your mother wasn't here. She could have taught the Indians about God." The boys nodded solemnly as they visualized their mother reading the Bible to little Indian boys and girls.

The road to Punta de Agua was less traveled than the road to Mountainair, and the car bumped slowly along for five more miles before they reached the outskirts of the town. Mardee then stopped so they could walk to the ruins. They had gone only a short distance when they spotted the ruins in a low ravine.

"It looks like a castle!" Roy exclaimed.

"I'm sure it really looked like a castle when it was built," Mardee said. "The walls were very high. Some have fallen down, but as you can see, some of the original walls are still standing. They were built of red sandstone cemented together with mud. The walls are very thick, from three to six feet through. That is why so much of the mission still stands."

The boys ran on ahead and entered the large portion that had been the church. Some of the 20-foot stone walls and large wooden beams were still visible. The structure had been built in the shape of the cross with the top of the cross containing the alter facing north. In Mardee's mind's eye, she could see many dark bowed heads filling the space and a religious man raising his arms in a silent blessing as he presided at the altar area. How magnificent! she thought. How wonderfully brave and dedicated these missionaries must have been.

Mardee knew from history that the Spanish missionaries had not always treated the Indians fairly as they taught them a new way of living and demanded their allegiance to a new God, but no one could doubt the courage of those pioneers.

Roy and John were now exploring the hallway that led to the living quarters. There were many rooms, probably some of them were for food storage, and they were all small, except those that were probably the priest's rooms. The boys ran happily through the maze of rooms, hiding and playing games.

Mardee got their attention. "You stay right here and play," she instructed. "Watch for snakes as Papa told you. I'll be back later. I'll honk from the road for you to come."

The boys waved happy goodbyes as they reveled in their freedom in this intriguing new environment. Mardee quickly walked to the car and drove the short distance into town. The adobe church was on the right side of the road as she drove up the main street, and people were starting to gather. Mardee parked the car on one side of the church and diverted her eyes from the newly dug hole in the cemetery.

As she got out of the car two men came to meet her, Frankie and an older man. "Welcome, Mardita," Frankie said quietly as she got out. "This is my father." He put his arm lightly around her waist.

The older man took Mardee's hand. "Thank you for coming, Miss Spencer." Although Frankie's father sometimes worked at the mill, Mardee had never really known him. He was tall and huskily built with a shock of gray hair, now freshly combed to the side and plastered down over his forehead. Mardee liked his shy smile and the direct blue-gray gaze of his eyes.

"My father could not come," she explained. "I am representing our family, and my mother sends her sympathy."

Mr. Moseby lowered his head and nodded his thanks.

"Let's go in the church now," Frankie said as he offered Mardee his arm.

As they entered, the cool church was a welcome relief from the heat of the day. The thick adobe walls kept the church comfortable even on the hottest summer days. Mardee was aware of curious glances as Frankie led them to the front of the church where the wooden coffin rested below the altar. Mardee had never seen anyone who had died other than her grandmother, and she was struck by the smooth peaceful face of Frankie's mother. She was beautiful, Mardee thought. Frankie has her dark coloring and her even features, but he is built like his father. No wonder he is so handsome!

The father and son paid their last respects to the woman who was so far removed from them now, and Frankie led them to a bench in the front row. "Your mother was a lovely woman," Mardee whispered as she sat down on the hard seat.

"Yes," Frankie answered with a sigh. "She was the prettiest girl on the Rio Grande when my father married her."

A long line of people soon streamed in the church and up to the casket. Some paid their respects quietly, some with tears and emotion.

Mardee's eyes filled with tears. She knew some of the tears were for Frankie's mother, but most of them were for her beloved grandmother whose memory always brought feelings of pain. She tried to take her mind off these emotions by looking around the church.

She had never been in a real place of worship before. When traveling preachers came to Eastview, they held services in her father's commissary.

People sat on rough benches that had been brought in while a man stood before them alternately reading the Bible, singing, praying, and berating them for their sins. Mardee never really enjoyed these services, because somehow, she just didn't feel as guilty as the speaker tried to make her feel. She believed in God and prayed to him often, but her God was loving and forgiving, not a condemning and vengeful one. She knew Sadie questioned the sincerity of her beliefs and was always trying to convert her, but she couldn't quite accept her stepmother's idea of worshipping.

Mardee marveled at the ornate altar, the rich gold cross on the wall, the images that decorated the walls and corner niches of the room, and the candles that flickered on a table in an alcove. The priest's words and movements were all foreign to her. She couldn't understand most of what he said, and she wondered how the people knew when to stand and when to kneel. But even though most of the words meant nothing to her, she found a feeling of peace and well-being slowly pervading her body. She prayed her own prayer when the people knelt, and she asked God to be with Frankie and his father. She also asked God to be with her and help her through the coming days of change and adjustment. She knew a new life away from home was going to be difficult.

She couldn't bring herself to think about Jeff and what might develop. The thought of being near him and able to see him and be with him brought sharp pangs of excitement, but she didn't want to think about what could happen in too much detail.

For now, she just sat in relaxed reflection until Frankie gently touched her shoulder. They walked out as a guitarist sang a Spanish song in a sorrowful voice.

As the people stood by the graveside the priest sprinkled holy water on the casket, and more foreign words were spoken. The casket was then lowered into the new grave, and Frankie and his father tossed the first shovels of earth on the casket, and then the grave was slowly filled with the remaining dirt.

Frankie led Mardee away from the grave site as Mr. Moseby followed, looking gray and shaken. Frankie turned to comfort him. "It's all right. You did the best you could for her. She loved you very much. She gave up her old life for you because she loved you. It was a hard change for her. Never feel sorry, Papa. She gave me to you and you to me. We must always remember that and be grateful to her because we have each other."

"I know, mi hito," came the broken answer. "I just feel so bad because I couldn't make her happy. I never knew what to do."

"You gave her all your love, Papa," Frankie persisted. "The demonios that haunted her life were not of your making." He gave his father a hug. "I will walk with Mardita for a while, and then I'll be home later."

As they headed for the car, Frankie said, "Thank you for coming. It means much to me to have you here."

"I'm glad I came." Mardee said softly. "Your mother was very beautiful. Heaven is prettier now because she is there."

Frankie took the crank, and the car started after a few turns. "Could you ride along with me?" Mardie said. "I left the boys at the ruins while I came to the funeral. I have something I want to tell you."

"Of course," Frankie said as he got in. "I guess I trust your driving," he added teasingly, smiling at her pretended scowl. "You know how hummingbirds are, mi hita. They fly around pretty fast searching for honey. I don't know how safe I am with you." He laughed suddenly, and Mardee realized how good it was to see him smile again.

"I'm just a dove today," she said lightly, "flying carefully and slowly. I must be a good driver for my little brothers and for you, my dear friend."

"Thank you," Frankie stated with mock seriousness. "Now what were you going to talk with me about?"

Mardee kept her eyes on the road. "I'm leaving soon for Santa Fe. I'm going to work there as an interpreter and also take some classes at the Loretta Academy."

Frankie said nothing for a few moments. "You're going to be with Jeff," he said with a sigh. "I don't want you to go, querida."

"Frankie, I'm excited about going. I'm excited about working and earning my own money. And I know it is a good idea to get more education."

Frankie nodded slowly. "Yes, my little one who loves life, you will enjoy all that. And I suppose you have a right to want it. But I'm afraid you don't know what you are getting into."

"There's one way to find out," Mardee said cheerfully. Then, more seriously, she added, "But Frankie, I've got to find out what's over these mountains, you know."

"I know, Mardita. But promise me that if you have any problems you will call me."

At that moment they arrived at the ruins, and Frankie helped her out of the car and pulled her close. "I will come to rescue you, my little paloma, if you break your wing." He then looked into her blue-green eyes and kissed her with an urgency she had never felt before, and she found herself responding to his passion. She anxiously attempted to pull back, but he held her tightly. "I will miss you, querida. Think of me once in a while, and say a prayer for me. I will be taking some classes myself to learn how to do my new job. It is harder than repairing track in the railroad yards."

Mardee looked up into his brooding dark eyes and smiled. "Why do you need prayers? Are you afraid you will not pass your tests?"

"I know I will pass," Frankie replied, kissing her forehead playfully. "But I could use some prayers." He then looked intently into her face. "You know, Mardita, my mother could never understand why she was different from everyone else. Her mother was Indian; her father was Mexican. She was never accepted by the Indians because she had a Mexican father. She was never accepted by the Mexicans because she was part Indian. Then she married an Anglo, and they never accepted her, either. But she found a place where she could go and drown her feelings of hurt. When she drank she was as good as anyone else, so she drank more and more until she killed herself. You remind me of her a little, mi hita. As Kurt Mason said in his song, 'Don't go into the fire as you sing and fly and search the world for the bittersweet honey you desire.'"

"I understand what you are saying," Mardee said thoughtfully. "I do feel different from other people, sometimes. My mother was part Indian. No one in my family has much use for Indians. Yet I am part of her, so I can't deny my heritage. Sometimes I feel a little hurt and confused." Her expressive eyes clouded for a moment, but then brightened as she quickly added, "But not for very long. I am going to make myself have a wonderful life."

By now the boys had spotted the car, and they came running over, both talking at once. "We found arrowheads!" John proclaimed loudly. "We had so much fun! Can we come here again, Mardee?"

"I imagine so, my little brothers," Mardee replied as they piled into the car. But she knew this was probably a promise she wouldn't keep as she looked into Frankie's accusing eyes, wordlessly reminding her that she was leaving. An empty feeling came over her, and she jumped in the car and abruptly gunned the motor, not looking back.

Frankie stood watching as the car disappeared in a cloud of dust. "When will I see you again, mi querida? Dios, what a day of sadness. Ya mi madre paso. Mi querida is also leaving me. Ay, Dios!" The tears that had been dammed up all day flowed freely.

13

The Model T chugged steadily over the dusty rough road as Ben Spencer drove Mardee to Santa Fe. Afterward, he would go on to Ojo Caliente for a few days. He had heard about the hot mineral baths that were supposed to help rheumatism. In cold weather his joints hurt almost unbearably, sometimes causing him to have to slack off on his work. And it was a good time to really test his new automobile, he had thought.

They had left the ranch after an early breakfast, and Ben had chosen a route which was shorter than going by Albuquerque. They went through Mountainair and Willard and then turned north to Estancia. Estancia was the county seat of Torrance County, and Ben had stopped at the courthouse to do some business. Then they headed for Moriarty, a small town which had grown up on the main road going from Albuquerque to Amarillo, where they refueled and filled up a five gallon gas can in case they needed it.

They bought cold drinks and took a few minutes to eat the sandwiches Sadie had sent with them. Mardee felt like a world traveler as she sat on a bench outside the gas station eating her lunch and watching the traffic go by. She was amazed at how many vehicles there were. She hadn't known there were so many cars in the whole world.

Ben soon got up from the bench and tossed the remains of his lunch in a garbage can. "Let's go, dear," he said. "We're making good time, and if we have no flats we can be in Santa Fe by early afternoon."

Mardee was glad to get back on the road, but realized that she had never before been this far from home. The landscape was now flat and arid; ahead and to the sides one could see nothing and more nothingness. As she glanced back she could dimly recognize the outline of her mountains rising majestically against the flatlands.

The mountain range stretched along the horizon for many miles, rising gently from low hills in the south to impressive peaks. The range built to its highest elevation, Manzano Peak, which was over 10,000 feet high. Capilla Peak rose to over 9,000 feet.

Mardee had once climbed to the top of this rugged giant. The terrain had been too steep for Gypsy, so she had ridden part way up and then climbed the rest of the way on foot. The view had been breathtaking as she looked down on the very land she and her father were now traveling. How long will it be before I get back to my mountains? she thought.

This momentous day was full of contradictions for Mardee. Her excitement about leaving home was tempered by the sadness of leaving her family. She loved her brothers and telling them goodbye had cut the emotional girl to the quick. For a moment as she had held Roy tightly, she thought, I can't do this. I can't leave my home.

Roy's sad eyes looking up at her had asked why. She could not answer that question from this little boy she loved so much. She had only hugged him tighter while the other boys crowded around her.

Even leaving Sadie was hard, and she knew she would miss her well-meant guidance. "Thanks for everything, Mother Spencer," she had said, "especially the pretty dress you made me."

Ox Canyon should be about there, Mardee thought as they bumped along, and there is home. She tried to pinpoint a canyon on the side of the mountain that pointed to the ranch. In her mind, she visualized Sadie and the children at the school house, the mill buzzing along, and Lola busily doing the chores. This is washday, she reminded herself, and was secretly happy that she wasn't there tending to the washpot and scrubbing work clothes on the wash board.

Mardee envisioned Gypsy running friskily in the pasture and kicking up her hooves. Quick tears came as she realized her riding days were over for a while, at least with Gypsy. I'll get Jeff to find me a horse to ride, she quickly promised herself and then felt better. But she knew no horse could ever replace Gypsy. Mardee had often poured out her heart to the loving animal and received comfort and understanding from the soft brown eyes. I couldn't have made it without you, Gypsy, she thought.

Then Mardee thought of her grandmother lying under the big yellow pine. You promised you would always be with me, you know. You promised.

Mardee's thoughts were interrupted by her father's loud voice. "Damn it to hell, anyway!" The car pulled to the side of the road and slowed to a stop. "I knew we'd been too lucky ," Ben said. "Let's fix this tire."

Ben found rocks and pushed them tightly in front of the three good wheels so the car wouldn't move as he jacked up the offending wheel. In a few minutes he was taking the tube out of the tire and examining the already patched tube carefully. At first he couldn't find a hole, but after spitting on it and watching for air bubbles, he finally found where the air was escaping.

"I can fix this in no time," he decreed as his good humor returned. "We'll save the spare tire for another time." He roughed the surface around the hole, put glue and a patch over it, and let the patch set for a few minutes before replacing the tube in the tire. Then with a hand pump he briskly pumped air into the tube, and before long the wheel was ready. The whole process took less than an hour.

Putting the jack back in its place and brushing the sand off his clothes, Ben pulled out his gold watch. "Now we are in good shape. We should be in Santa Fe by three o'clock."

If we don't have another flat tire, Mardee thought.

The road to Santa Fe led through Stanley, a small prairie town, and then Galisteo, an old Spanish village. The country was now changing to high mountain mesas dotted with scrub cedars, and the Sangre de Cristos rose to the north.

Mardee breathed a sigh of relief. "Look at those mountains! I couldn't exist in this flatland. I would die!" she announced dramatically.

"Well, you won't die if it's mountains that will keep you alive," Ben said dryly. "Santa Fe lies in the foothills of those impressive peaks."

Mardee's eyes had become heavy, but just as she was drifting off to sleep her father's voice jerked her sagging head to attention. He was pointing to a group of Indians kneeling around a prostrate animal.

"What are they doing?" Mardee asked nervously.

"Butchering a horse," Ben answered. "And they are salvaging the meat."

"For what?" Mardee asked.

"To eat," Ben answered. "They'll split it up and carry it home in a skin pack on the back of their horses. There'll be great feasting in their pueblo tonight."

Mardee's face carried a frown of distaste. She did not want to think of any horse being eaten.

Ben tried to explain. "The horse will either be eaten by the animals or by the Indians. Better the Indians; they need the food." Mardee knew her father was right.

The Indians were soon left behind as the little car labored up a long steep hill. Ben anxiously watched his radiator cap for steam. "We're on the Lamy Hill," he said tightly. "This is our last bad hill before we get to Santa Fe."

Once they were at the top the driver breathed a sigh of relief. "Lamy lies in that direction." Ben gestured to the east. "It's a railroad town named for Archbishop Lamy."

"Who is he?" Mardee asked.

"A Catholic priest who came to New Mexico in the 1800's. He was the first archbishop for the Archdiocese of Santa Fe. That means he was head of all the Catholic Churches in the area, and there were many of them because of the Spanish exploration of the southwest. Sadie discounts the Catholic Church, but it's just because she doesn't appreciate its importance in New Mexico history."

Ben's gray eyes swept over the terrain. He loved to travel and view new country. His sharp eyes took in the fact that this was not good timber land. The scrub cedar would only be good for fence posts. It was not good grazing land, either. The soil was too rocky, and the rainfall was probably light.

Continuing, he said, "Bishop Lamy was a sophisticated priest from France, and he was sent by the Pope, who is the head of the Catholic Church all over the world, to help tame what they considered the rough and godless citizens of this far western Catholic outpost. Bishop Lamy had the magnificent Saint Francis Cathedral built according to his refined European tastes. It's close to the plaza in Santa Fe, the most impressive structure I've ever seen. You will be thrilled with it because you love beautiful things."

Mardee stared at her father with wide eyes. She was surprised at his knowledge of the history of Catholicism. "Is Pastor Lamy at the Manzano Catholic Church related to Archbishop Lamy?" she asked.

"Yes," her father answered. "He's a nephew, and well loved by his flock."

Mardee admired her father because he had been so many places and done so many different things. She knew he viewed life from a broader perspective than most people, and this influenced his thoughts and beliefs. That's why she could trust him. There had never been a time in her life when she didn't trust her father to know best.

She looked at him admiringly. "Papa, thank you for taking me to Santa Fe. Thank you for letting Jeff get me a job with the governor. And thank you for letting me go to the Academy. I am so excited about going to school again.You've done so much for me."

Ben glanced over at her. "You are an outstanding daughter, dear." he said as he turned his eyes to the road. "You have been a good student and a good helper. Wherever you go, you bring love and warmth. You have been our own private ray of sunshine. We will miss you. I will miss you most of all." Ben cleared his throat as he kept his eyes firmly on the road.

"Let me drive, Papa," she said quickly to dispel her emotion. "You must be tired."

Ben slowed down. "I am tired," he said. "My back hurts. You're a better driver than I am, anyway."

"I think I am a very lucky girl," she said ecstatically as she walked around to get in the driver's seat.

Mardee hesitated a moment as she looked back to the southwest. Quickly sliding into the car as her father moved into the passenger seat, she thought, Goodbye, Manzanos. Hello, Sangre de Cristos!

14

I can't wait to see Jeff! I can't wait to feel his arms around me. I'll be in Santa Fe tonight! All thoughts of home had vanished.

The narrow road leading into Santa Fe wound its way between small adobe homes to come to an end at the plaza, a common area around which all Spanish towns were constructed. "There's the Palace of the Governors," Ben gestured. "That's the Precidio Building behind which houses the soldiers who protect the governor. Park right there in front of that door. Governor McDonald's office is just inside."

Mardee quickly stepped down from the car, took a deep breath, straightened her dress, and smoothed her hair. She then followed her father to a massive wooden doorway and entered as he held the door for her. Inside was a waiting area for the governor's visitors. She stared at the wide whitewashed walls crowned by gleaming log vigas in the ceiling.

"I am Ben Spencer, and this is my daughter, Mardee. We wish to see Governor McDonald." Ben said to the young man at the desk.

The governor's aide vanished through a short wide door behind him and returned almost immediately. "The governor will see you," he said with a smile, his young eyes lingering on Mardee.

Ben took Mardee's arm as they walked through the door. A distinguished man rose from behind a desk and walked briskly around to greet them. He shook hands with her father, and she extended her hand to his warm clasp. She looked up into deep blue eyes and a friendly smile camouflaged by a gray mustache. "I am so happy to meet you, sir," she said earnestly with a slight smile.

Mardee and her father were then seated in elaborately carved chairs facing the governor. The two men spoke in easy conversation about their days together in White Oaks. "Remember when the sheriff came to your mill to buy lumber to build a scaffold to hang the 'Kid,' and by the time he got back to Lincoln his prisoner had broken out of jail?" the governor said. His eyes twinkled and the two friends laughed together as they thought of the early days in White Oaks.

Mardee looked curiously around the governor's office. It was a plain room, sparsely decorated. A heavy woolen rug covered most of the wooden floor and a small niche cut in one of the adobe walls held a religious statue and a cross.

"I appreciate your willingness to give my daughter a job in your office," Ben said. "As I told you, she speaks the Spanish language fluently, having been raised in the Manzanos with mostly Spanish children for playmates. Not only does she know and understand the language, she understands the people. She should be good help to you in many areas."

"Yes," the governor said thoughtfully, "not being a native myself, I can use someone with her skills. And knowing her father as I do makes me confident that I can depend on her. It will work out perfectly for me to have her here part-time, as I don't have the budget for any more full-time help."

"It works out well for us, too," Ben said. "I want her to have more education, and I have made arrangements with the Loretta Academy for her to attend classes in the morning. She will study Spanish composition, typing, and English. Those courses should help her with her duties here. She will be staying with Judge Roberts and his wife on Grant Street, only two blocks from here, so she will be living close to school and work."

"Sounds like a good arrangement," the governor agreed, nodding. Turning to Mardee, he addressed her for the first time. "Miss Spencer, you will also be helping out in other offices if they need you. I welcome you to this office, and I look forward to a pleasant and worthwhile association."

Ben rose and extended his hand to the governor. "Thank you so much, Bill. It means a great deal to me for my daughter to have this opportunity. I am forever indebted to you."

The governor smiled at his old friend. "I am happy to be able to do this for your daughter. I know she will be an asset to my administration."

Turning to Mardee, he bowed slightly. "See you tomorrow, my dear."

Mardee's face flushed with pleasure at her new situation, and as her father took her arm, she managed to say, "Thank you, sir. I'll look forward to seeing you tomorrow."

When Mardee and Ben emerged from the governor's office, a tall familiar figure rose to greet them. "Welcome to Santa Fe," Jeff Corbin said.

Mardee quickly reached out to this man who had been in her thoughts for so many months and as she drowned in his amused blue eyes, she murmured, "This is a day of miracles, and you are the biggest one of all!"

"You are the miracle, Mardee," he replied softly. "There has never been a woman who looked like you in this office before. The soldiers spotted you as you drove up, and they called you an angel from heaven. But I think not," Jeff smiled. "Just a mountain goddess from the Manzanos!"

Giving her a quick hug, Jeff turned to Ben as Mardee stood in numbed silence. "How are you, Ben?" Jeff asked warmly. "It is good to see you. I thought you would never get here. I have been waiting for hours."

"Waiting for me or for Mardee?" Ben asked wryly, but he relaxed and took Jeff's hand with pleasure. "It's good to see you, Jeff. You look well."

Mardee, now recovered from her first sight of Jeff, interrupted, "Yes, he graces these hallowed halls very handsomely, don't you think, Papa?"

Ben looked from his young lawyer friend to his pretty daughter and was stunned by the striking picture they made. Dangerously so, he thought. Then, almost brusquely, he said, "Mardee, we must go talk to Sister Evangelina about your classes."

Jeff said quickly, "I know you have things to do, but I would like to take you both to dinner tonight. And Ben, I want you to spend the night with me so you don't have to get a hotel room."

"That's very kind of you, Jeff," Ben slowly replied. "I've made housing arrangements at the Roberts' for Mardee, but nothing for myself, yet. Of course, it will be for one night only. I plan to go on to Ojo Caliente tomorrow.

I will be there for about a week to take the mineral baths. My rheumatism has been giving me fits lately."

"Very well, Ben. I'll pick you both up at the Roberts' house later. See you then."

She's going to brighten this place up, Jeff thought with satisfaction as he watched Ben and Mardee disappear down the street.

15

As they entered the large plain school, Mardee felt an instant sense of belonging. They passed quiet rooms where girlish heads were bent over books and tablets as a faint scent of chalk permeated the air. Nuns in black habits moved silently among the students.

Mardee felt almost overwhelmed in this school that consisted of more than one room. Pictures of Jesus and Mary and various saints of the church looked down on them as they continued down the hall, wooden floors gleaming beneath their feet. She realized this was not only a place of learning, but also a House of God. Maybe I can find Sadie's God easier here, she thought.

Soon they came to a door with the sign, Sister Evangelina, Principal. Mardee was surprised when the sister greeted her father warmly. "Ben Spencer, it's been so long . It's so good to see you again, and especially since you are bringing us your daughter!"

Sister Evangelina clasped Mardee's small hands tightly in her own large soft ones, making Mardee feel at ease. Soon father and daughter were talking excitedly about their trip and their anticipation of Mardee being a student in the Academy. "Mardee is a good student and eager to learn. I think you will be pleased with her performance," Ben said.

"We will expect nothing less," Sister Evangelina replied. "Of course," she added, "our students are all full-time and live here in the dormitory, but for you, Ben Spencer, and our good friend, Governor McDonald, we are making this exception." She winked at Ben as she smiled in Mardee's direction.

Ben then expressed his gratitude, paid the tuition, and arranged for the uniforms Mardee would wear to class. She would attend three classes and a study hall, starting the next morning.

Before they left Sister Evangelina took the new student and her father to the chapel. "We expect all our students to attend Mass once a week, Mardee, and even though you are not Catholic, we will want you here with the other students. I think you will enjoy it, and later, if you want to sing in the choir we will talk to Sister Rita about that."

As Mardee looked around the Loretta Chapel she stood speechless, gazing up at the high arched ceiling and magnificent stained glass windows. Her eyes moved to the white marble alter with three spires behind it, six candles on either side, and a gold cross in the middle. When her eyes fell on the statues of Mary on the left of the alter and Jesus on the right, tears streamed down her cheeks. She instinctively clasped her hands in prayer and whispered softly, "Thank you, God. This is so beautiful."

Sister Evangelina gently turned Mardee around. "The choir sings up there," she said, pointing to the balcony at the rear of the church. "Notice the circular staircase that goes up to the loft. I must get back to my office, but have your father tell you the story about the staircase. I told him about it once. I'm sure he remembers." With a final clasp of the hand she told Ben goodbye and gave Mardee a quick pat on the shoulder.

Mardee took the clean handkerchief Sadie had thrust in her pocket that morning and wiped her wet cheeks. "Tell me the story, Papa."

As Ben and Mardee sat down on a hard slick church bench, Ben remembered his reaction the first time he had seen this chapel. He had come here one evening on one of his business trips. Before starting back to White Oaks he had stepped into this quiet haven to meditate. His personal life with Mardee's mother wasn't going well, and he needed help. That was when he had met Sister Evangelina. She had sat quietly beside him and asked if she could pray for him. He had poured out his anxieties to this kind woman and found comfort in her steadfast faith and compassion. He never forgot her last words to him that night, "Remember, we are all part of God's Great Plan. Sometimes we don't understand why things happen, but we must always have faith that God is watching over us, and everything will work out in the end." Ever since then Ben had stopped to see Sister Evangelina and spend some time in the Loretta Chapel when he was in Santa Fe.

Bringing his mind back to the present, he turned to Mardee and explained that the Loretta Chapel was built for the girls who attended the Loretta Academy. As the young girl listened with wide eyes he told her how Bishop Lamy had the chapel constructed in 1873 and had wanted the Sisters of Loretta to have a chapel that was similar to his beloved Sainte Chapelle in Paris, which was a Gothic structure. So the Loretta Chapel became the first Gothic structure west of the Mississippi.

"How proud the bishop must have been of this chapel!" Mardee interrupted.

Ben then told her that there was one flaw in this beautiful structure. "There was no way to get up to the choir loft. The builders had assumed that ladders would be used, but the loft was very high, and the sisters didn't want the girls to climb high ladders. So they called in carpenters to see if they could construct stairs, but each said it couldn't be done. It would require too much room to build stairs to such a height.

"But," Ben continued, "the Sisters of Loretta did not give up. Since Saint Joseph was their patron saint, they made a novena to him for a suitable solution. On the ninth day of their prayers a grayhaired man appeared with a donkey and a tool chest. He offered to help the sisters build the stairway.

"The carpenter worked with only a saw, a hammer, and a T square, and countless tubs of hot water to curve the lumber. It took months for the carpenter to build a staircase twenty-three and one-half feet high with thirty-three steps. There were two 360 degree turns, and no center supports. Only the perfection of its craftsmanship kept it from collapsing then, and the same is true to this day.

"But," Ben said in a mysterious voice, "when the Mother Superior went to pay the carpenter, he had vanished. And when she went to the local lumber yard to pay for the wood there was no record that any wood had been bought." Ben paused. "It is still a mystery where the old carpenter got the wood."

"I think only God knows how it got there," Mardee said as they rose to leave.

They then made their way to the Roberts home where the judge and his wife, Addie, welcomed the tired travelers with open arms. Ben and the judge hit it off immediately, and Mardee followed Addie to the kitchen to help prepare the evening meal. Jeff arrived shortly, and Mrs. Roberts insisted that he join them for dinner. She assured him that her pork chops and apple pie would taste much better than the food in some cafe.

Jeff readily accepted, looking forward to a good homecooked meal.

In a short time dinner was ready and the judge presided. He was a jovial man with blue eyes and a handlebar mustache that twitched while he laughed the hardest of anyone over his tales. His wife smiled indulgently at her husband's stories as she piled more food on the table.

After dinner the men talked a while in the judge's office, and then Jeff and Ben took their leave. Mardee kissed her father goodbye, smiled at Jeff, and went to the kitchen to help with the dishes. Mrs. Roberts noticed the tears sparkling on her dark eyelashes and gave her a hug as she handed her a dish towel. "You will miss your father, dear, but we promised him we would take good care of you. You will enjoy life here. I just know you will." Mardee's tears subsided. As Sadie had always said, her tears came easily and dried quickly.

After the kitchen was clean Mardee was happy to retire to her little room at the end of the second floor hall. Before getting ready for bed Mardee walked silently down the hall and peered out the big window that faced the street and overlooked the town. The moon was so bright she could see the bushes and shade trees and green grass. She had never seen grass in a yard before. The yard at home was bare and hard from the many busy people walking and running over the ground all the time. I'll take a book and lie in the grass under that big elm tree and read sometime, she promised herself.

Mardee remembered her father had told her about this colonial style home that had been constructed about ten years ago. It had three stories and was made of wood and brick with large windows and shiny polished hardwood floors. Mardee had never imagined that homes could be this fancy. "I'm the luckiest girl in the world," she told herself for the second time on this exciting day as she looked out at the long anticipated lights of Santa Fe.

16

Jeff quickly left his apartment house and headed for Grant Street. He was excited about escorting Mardee to the annual fiesta that commemorated the return of the Spanish to Santa Fe after the Indians had chased them out during the Indian Revolt in 1680.

Under the leadership of Don Diego de Vargas the Spanish had reclaimed Santa Fe in 1692, and this time they were there to stay. Every year since the town celebrated with a fiesta marking this important time in its history. A carved sixteenth century wooden statue of the Virgin Mary, brought by the Spaniards when they triumphantly returned, was proudly paraded annually.

Jeff had kept a close eye on Mardee during her first week in Santa Fe. She had been given a small office near young John Weeks, the governor's aide. John was her supervisor. She assisted him in translating Spanish correspondence for the governor, as well as helping write the responses in Spanish. Sometimes she acted as interpretor between the governor and his Spanish visitors. John arranged for Mardee to assist anyone who needed help with interpretation or composition of Spanish.

By the time Mardee had arrived at her desk on the first afternoon John already had a full schedule of tasks lined out for her. She enjoyed the work because it was easy for her, and because she found most of the people very interesting.

Her co-workers quickly realized that this pretty young girl was extremely capable. Many of the governor's staff were not native to New Mexico, and they found Mardee's knowledge of her state and its people helpful. Governor McDonald gratefully expressed his appreciation to Jeff for being instrumental in getting her there.

As Jeff hurried past the fiesta activity in the plaza he realized how pleased he felt at being able to take Mardee out for the first time alone. He had tried to convince himself that he was only helping Ben when he arranged a job for Mardee and found a place for her to stay. Having been away from her for a while, her compelling charm had somewhat abated, and he had resumed his correspondence and plans with Heather. He was an ambitious young man, and he knew that marrying Heather would be a smart step. This would cement his position with the influential men who were designing the political profile of New Mexico.

He was fond of Heather. She was a lovely well-educated young woman who would be a definite asset for his future. But now Jeff felt a moment of anxiety as he sensed the quandary he had brought upon himself. However, he thrust these thoughts aside as he walked up to the front door and firmly lifted the knocker.

Addie Roberts quickly appeared and led Jeff to Judge Roberts' office. "Have a seat here, Jeff," she said, smiling. "The judge is performing a wedding, and Mardee wanted to observe. He should be finished any minute. Excuse me, and I will get back to my kitchen."

Jeff sat down, and from where he was sitting he had a good view of the proceedings across the hall. The judge and the young couple and their attendants stood in the middle of the room. An older couple with somber expressions sat on a settee on one side of the room. They don't look too pleased, Jeff noted.

The judge soon finished and smilingly shook hands with the couple. He then led the wedding party to a table and pointed to papers they were to sign. He congratulated them again, and everyone turned to leave. Jeff was startled to see the mother's face crumple into tears as she walked out the door.

Mardee and the judge then came into the office, and Judge Roberts put the papers in his desk. "I'll get those filed tomorrow in the courthouse," he remarked to Mardee. "Hello, Jeff," he said as he turned to the young man. "Sorry we're late, but we had some complications." He winked at Mardee.

Mardee wore a long brightly printed skirt with a sheer blouse draped becomingly over her youthful body. The top two buttons of her blouse were unfastened, and the milky whiteness of her throat and upper bosom rose appealingly from its folds. "I've just seen my very first wedding, Jeff," she said, her face pink with excitement. "It was so interesting, but Judge, why was everyone so serious? And why did the bride keep running outside during the ceremony?"

The judge smiled at Mardee and said gently, "I don't think she felt well. She was very nervous." The judge twirled one end of his handle-bar mustache thoughtfully and added, "The groom was nervous, too, over this shotgun wedding."

"Shotgun wedding," Mardee repeated. "What do you mean, Judge Roberts?"

The judge's eyes twinkled. "Why, child, didn't you see that shotgun the father was holding?"

"I didn't see any shotgun," Mardee replied with alarm.

Judge Roberts quickly looked over at Jeff. "I'm going to have my supper which was delayed because of this wedding. You and Mardee go out and have fun, and maybe you can explain this for me. But have her home by midnight."

"Yes sir," Jeff answered as he took Mardee's arm. "Good night, sir."

"Well, Jeff?" she demanded as they headed down the front walk.

"How's my girl from the mountains?" he asked, ignoring her questioning eyes. "How's my Mardeebird?" He suddenly felt a hot rush of desire to possess those pouting lips. "You are so beautiful tonight, my dear. I'm glad you came to Santa Fe. You are going to enjoy this fiesta. We will dance and eat and sing and have fun!"

Mardee then moved quickly in front of her escort and planted her feet on the sidewalk, arms on her hips. "Jeff, you are avoiding my question. What is a shotgun wedding?"

Jeff sighed and said in a resigned voice, "Mardee, do you know what being in the family way means?"

"Yes," she replied quickly. "It means you are going to have a baby."

"Well," Jeff continued, "that bride was in that condition. That's why she was always running outside. She was nervous and nauseated."

A slight smile appeared on Mardee's face. "I see," she murmured, and then laughter escaped in a merry outburst. "I'm sorry I put you in an embarrassing situation. But I think I'm more sorry for those poor people." Then, pointing her small finger at him, she admonished, "Always remember that you can tell me anything. I'm no baby."

"True," Jeff concurred and averted his eyes from the tantalizing picture of desire she posed for him. To himself he added, Certainly no baby. A full-blown temptress, yes!

As they slowly walked on toward the fiesta lights Mardee told Jeff about her week.

"So you have learned a great deal in these few days?" Jeff asked. "More than just about a shotgun wedding?"

Mardee looked up at him with a mock scowl as they moved in and out among the people on the plaza . "I will ignore that reference," she said primly, and then with enthusiasm she added, "At school there is much to learn. Luckily, Mother Spencer gave me good English instruction so I'm doing fine in that class, but the assignments are long. Typing is coming along well. I had actually learned to type on my father's old Smith typewriter in his office, so I will soon be able to do all my own typing, and John won't have to help me out so much. Spanish composition is my most difficult subject because we also learn spelling along with the writing, and the Spanish vowels have different sounds than the English vowels. Some of the consonants have different sounds, too, like the letter J sounds like an H in Spanish. But I know the vocabulary already, and I'll learn the grammar and the spelling quickly. It's really fun to be learning new things."

Mardee smiled up at Jeff and laughed just for the joy of it. But she quickly caught herself. "Another thing I learned this week was not to laugh so often and so loudly. Sister Bernice reminds me constantly to keep my laughter down. I must do everything more quietly. Mother Spencer would love this teacher!"

"You're perfect as far as I'm concerned," Jeff assured her, holding her hand tighter. "Don't let her squelch you too much."

They were now in the center of the plaza where Spanish music was dominating the festivities. Trumpets blared the familiar Spanish melodies, violins sweetly joined the loud horns, and guitars deftly carried the beat. One could not hear this music without dancing, and Jeff quickly swept his mountain girl into his arms. They whirled to the music in wild exhileration. They danced to everything; the two steps, the schottisches, the waltzes, and the Spanish dances. Everyone made room for them to perform the Mexican Hat Dance as Jeff tossed his widebrimmed hat to the ground, and Mardee held her skirts and stamped rhythmically around it. The tall blonde Gringo and his pretty little senorita was a sight that caught many admiring eyes.

After the dance they drifted to one side of the plaza and sat down at one of the tables for biscochitas and lemonade. "I'm so hot and tired!" Mardee exclaimed with a smile.

"Maybe you're just a little out of practice, Mardee," Jeff said teasingly.

"Don't think that you're the only dancing partner I've had lately," Mardee replied. "I danced all night not long ago at our harvest dance, and there was certainly no lack of partners that night."

Jeff took a long drink of cool lemonade, leaned back, and looked at Mardee through half-closed eyes. After a quiet sigh he remarked, "No, I'm sure there were lots of partners. But if I had been there, your one partner would have been me!"

"Maybe," Mardee said thoughtfully. "But Kurt wouldn't have liked that, and neither would Frankie."

Two wandering guitar players suddenly interrupted their banter with the lilting notes of *La Cucharacha*. Mardee jumped up, saying to Jeff, "Venga, mi querida, canta y no llores. Sing with me, don't cry over my boy friends!"

Mardee then sang the song as a crowd collected. When she finished Jeff put a firm arm around her waist and pulled her away from her admirers.

"Let's take a walk down by the river," Jeff suggested. "You've shown off enough for one night."

"All right, that suits me fine," Mardee smiled. "I'd rather be alone with you anyway, mi amigo."

The couple quickly walked the short distance to the Santa Fe River. It was more of a creek than a river, and the ripple of the waters circling the aspen trees and chokecherry bushes on the banks muted the raucous sounds of the fiesta. They sat down on a grassy knoll. Mardee nestled up against Jeff's broad chest and closed her eyes.

"Are you happy to be in Santa Fe?" Jeff whispered.

"So happy," was her answer. She then lifted her full sensual lips to Jeff. Their bodies slowly relaxed on the soft grassy mat as Jeff felt the alluring roundness of her body. His hands searched for forbidden treasures as their passions mounted.

"I love you, my little darling," he said softly in her ear. Jeff's demanding lips spread their hot magic down to her thrusting breasts. Piercing desire flooded her body as she arched up to meet his need. She opened her eyes briefly in awesome wonder and saw the stars bursting with joy and turning into rockets.

"Oh Jeff, my love," she whispered hoarsely.

Suddenly the night was shattered by explosives that changed their intimacy into chaos. "What the hell?" Jeff muttered as he looked around. More violent outbursts split the night air, one following closely on the other as rockets exploded in the sky.

"Of course, it's the fireworks," he said, shaking his head. "They were going to shoot them off at midnight. My God, Mardee, we've got to get out of here! I'm supposed to have you home by now."

17

Jeff quickly opened the door without knocking, and they headed straight to Judge Roberts' office. As they appeared in his door he raised his head, and before he could say a word Jeff blurted out, "Sorry we're late, sir." Lowering his head, he added lamely, "The time seemed to go by so fast."

"That's all right, Jeff," the judge replied, looking from a nervous Jeff to his red-cheeked companion. "I'll give you ten minutes leeway. I'm a fair man."

"Thank you, sir," Jeff said as he abruptly turned to leave. "Goodnight, Mardee."

As he let himself out Mardee said goodnight to the judge and hurriedly headed for the stairs. She took off her fiesta skirt and blouse and changed into her comfortable nightgown. After she had washed her face and brushed her tousled hair she fell into bed, and then the tears came. What did I do tonight? she asked herself. She finally fell into a fitful sleep, confused about her first evening with Jeff. She dreamed of rockets bursting in the sky and shotgun weddings.

The next morning the Robertses attended the Presbyterian Church not far from their home, and Mardee looked around her with interest as they sat on varnished hard benches. She noticed that the interior of the church was beautiful, but not so richly and colorfully designed as the school chapel. And when the choir marched in, their music seemed more melodious than the hymns at school.

Mardee was enjoying the service until the dignified minister stood at the pulpit and announced his text for his Sunday sermon: "Marriage is honorable among all, and the bed undefiled; but fornicators and adulterers God will judge!"

Mardee sat stiffly while marriage, fornicators, and adulterers were defined. As the sermon progressed, Mardee had the guilty feeling that the words were being directed straight at her. As the final hymn, *Just as I am*, was sung, Mardee prayed silently, Dear Lord, forgive me.

After a quiet walk home Mardee helped Mrs. Roberts set the table and slice the roast for dinner. Smells good, she thought. But the flavorful meat was difficult to swallow as she fought back a lump that had settled in her throat.

After the dishes were done Mardee quickly excused herself to do her homework. She had just settled down at her small desk and opened her English book when there was a soft knock on the door.

"I'm sorry to bother you," Mrs. Roberts said apologetically, "but I thought perhaps we could have a little talk before you start studying."

"Of course," Mardee answered uneasily.

"I guess I get lonesome for someone to talk to since my girls are married and gone. That's one reason I am so happy to have you here. It's so good to have a young girl in the house again."

"Well, I'm certainly glad to be here," Mardee said, smiling.

"We haven't talked too much about your family, Mardee," Mrs. Roberts continued. "Could you come sit here beside me on the bed and tell me all about them?"

"Oh yes," Mardee said, glad to be talking about her family.

Mrs. Roberts smiled. "I know you are very close to your father. I could tell that when he was here."

"Oh yes," Mardee said with enthusiasm. "He's the best father in the whole world."

"And your stepmother?" Mrs. Roberts asked gently.

"Mother Spencer is a good woman, a very religious woman. Sometimes I have a hard time being the way she thinks I should be."

"And does she talk to you?" Mrs. Roberts asked.

Mardee shook her head. "No, not really." Then she added, "But we did have a nice visit once. She even made me a lemon pie."

"So you like lemon pie? Well, I'll just plan to have lemon pie for dessert next Sunday."

"That would be nice," Mardee replied.

"And you have brothers, don't you?"

"There's Floyd, the oldest, who is thirteen years old, Charlie who is twelve, John who is ten years old, and Roy, the youngest, who is only eight." As she thought of little Roy, tears came to her eyes.

Mrs. Roberts held Mardee's head to her breast and stroked her forehead. "It's all right, dear. You're just a little homesick today."

"It's more than that, Mrs. Roberts," Mardee stammered as she blurted out, "I'm a fornicator, too."

"I doubt that very much, dear," Mrs. Roberts answered more calmly than she felt. "Do you even know what that word means?"

"Yes," Mardee said between sobs, "The minister explained it this morning. And it happened last night."

"With Jeff?" Mrs. Roberts asked.

Mardee nodded. Now that she had made her confession, the tears were slowing down.

"What did you do?" Mrs. Roberts asked firmly.

"I guess I fornicated," Mardee said quietly.

"But what exactly did you do? Did you kiss Jeff?" Mrs. Roberts pursued.

"Yes, I kissed him, and I never wanted to stop kissing him. I have never had such feelings in my body before. Mother Spencer told me that you mustn't let a boy go too far because that's how you get in the family way. I guess I'll have to have a shotgun wedding now!"

Mrs. Roberts patted her hand gently. "Mardee, did you do anything else besides kiss Jeff and experience strange feelings?"

Mardee shook her head sadly, "No, that's all I did, but that was too much."

Mrs. Roberts lifted Mardee's chin and looked directly into her eyes.

"Mardee, you and Jeff shared passionate kisses because there is a strong attraction between you. Your body responded in a passionate way. But you are not a fornicator. You are just an innocent young girl who likes a young man, perhaps a little too much. That's why you have to be careful, as your stepmother explained, and not let the situation go too far before the time is right for those actions. After marriage. Do you understand me, dear?"

Mardee looked into Mrs. Roberts' eyes as she asked slowly, "Are you sure we didn't let things get out of hand?"

"It may have gone farther than it should, but I am sure it didn't go too far." Mrs. Roberts said firmly. Then she hesitated and continued, "Now in the future, Mardee, you must use your good judgment. You know, men think they are the stronger of the two sexes, but I'll tell you a secret. Women are really the stronger. We are the ones who have to make sure that desire doesn't take over before it should." Mrs. Roberts looked thoughtfully at Mardee. "What did you learn last night, dear?" she asked gently.

"Romancing has to be controlled," Mardee summarized seriously. "I must use better judgment from now on. I must be strong."

"I know you will, Mardee," Mrs. Roberts assured her. "I have faith in you, and so does your father and your stepmother, or they would never have let you come here."

Mrs. Roberts gently got up from the bed. "Let's have these talks often, shall we?"

"Oh yes," Mardee answered, "but one more question before you leave. Do you think Jeff is angry with me about what happened?"

"Jeff is not angry with you. He cares for you deeply, I'm sure," Mrs. Roberts replied with a wise look. "Jeff would never do anything to hurt you. Don't worry about anything, dear. Everything is fine!"

Mrs. Roberts then smiled and softly closed the door behind her. Mardee fell over on her bed. Mrs. Roberts thinks we were the strong ones last night, she thought, but she doesn't know that the credit really goes to the fireworks!

18

Mardee walked briskly to school Monday morning, her weekend crisis settled in her mind. She now felt more grown-up and sure of herself. She had learned that being in love meant you must be cautious with your emotions.

As Mardee hurried down the hall to her English class Sister Bernice fell into step with her. She was a large nun whose broad face could mirror sadness or anger or happiness very expressively. This morning she looked beamingly pleasant as she asked Mardee about her weekend. "It was nice," Mardee replied sedately, adding to herself, if you only knew!

"Wonderful!" Sister Bernice smiled dramatically. "There's a question I want to ask you. How much of the old classics have you read?"

"Not much," Mardee answered. "We didn't have a library at my school in the mountains. But I did read the Bible often."

"That's good, but that's not the book I was thinking about. Have you ever heard of *Little Women* by Louisa Mae Alcott?"

Mardee shook her head.

"Well, it's a wonderful story set in the Civil War Era. It's about a mother and her four daughters and how they survive while the husband and father is away in the army."

"That sounds good," Mardee enthused.

"Check it out of the library today," Sister Bernice directed. "We are going to do the play, and you might be interested in trying out for one of the parts."

Mardee soon had the book in her hands and started reading it between her classes. The story gripped her right from the first page. What fun it would be to play any of these characters, she thought. Especially the brave mother!

Mardee felt a new world unfolding to her as she read. She knew very little about New England; it seemed as far away as China. But as she read, the area became real when she pictured the cold winter weather. And as some of the characters unfolded, she realized that real people very much like herself lived there. When I've finished this book, I will check out another, she promised herself.

That afternoon Mardee sat at her desk in the Governors Palace with a new sense of maturity. She spoke in a well modulated voice to her co-workers and smiled less effusively. She tried to behave the way the genteel Meg would if she had this job.

"Well, aren't you the grand one today!" John Weeks remarked as he approached Mardee's desk.

John hadn't held out much hope that she would be able to do this job efficiently at first. But she had surprised him with what she was able to do.

"I'll take that as a compliment," Mardee said sweetly.

"Oh yes, yes," John stuttered, slightly embarrassed. "Check with me when you get that letter done. I have a job I need your help on."

"Certainly, sir," Mardee replied, smiling as he left the room.

John had barely vanished when Jeff Corbin appeared in the doorway, his face strangely serious.

"Hello, Jeff!" Mardee exclaimed.

"Hello, Mardee," Jeff said quietly. "I must talk with you. I won't take up much time. I know you are busy."

"Of course," Mardee replied softly.

"I'm sorry," he began after he cleared his throat. "I'm sorry about what happened last night. I told your father I would take care of you. I should never have let things go so far."

Mardee looked up at the nervous young man, her eyes luminous. "Oh Jeff," she whispered, "don't be sorry. It was my fault, too."

Jeff looked down at this woman child, so mature in many ways, so childlike in matters of the heart. "Listen to me, Mardee," he said firmly, "this must not go on. I think too much of you."

"I understand, Jeff," Mardee said, nodding seriously. "I didn't know love could be so explosive."

"Explosive is the right word," Jeff said with a grin. "And thanks to the explosives, we escaped! You are too young, Mardee."

"Not too young to know I love you, Jeff," Mardee said with a break in her voice. "But I promise to be good in the future."

"Very well," Jeff said with relief. "I'm going to be gone for a while to the northern part of the state to do some work on the Spanish Land Grants. Be a good girl, but have a good time. Stewart over there at the Presidio wants to meet you."

"All right," Mardee said uneasily, wondering why Jeff wanted her to meet Stewart. She dared not think he wanted to get rid of her. "Send him over," she said brightly, in spite of any real enthusiasm.

"I'll do that," Jeff said quickly. "Goodbye, my dear." He took her hand and gave it a soft kiss. As he lifted his head and met her eyes she wondered if that was pain she glimpsed in his wavering glance.

"Goodbye, Jeff," she said with dry eyes and a crying heart.

Why am I always saying goodbye? she asked herself angrily. Then with an impatient shake of her head she admonished herself to be brave like the Marsh girls.

At that moment John stuck his head in the door. "The governor needs your help with a Spanish gentleman."

19

After work that afternoon, a young Spanish boy ran up to Mardee as she turned the corner to the Roberts' house. There was an expression of urgency on his face. She stopped and asked, "What do you want?"

He didn't respond, so she asked again, this time in Spanish, "Que quieres, muchacho?"

"Quiero a ver el juez," the boy answered quickly.

"Porque?" asked Mardee. "Why do you need to see the judge?"

"Porque mi madre esta muy enfirmo," the boy said, his voice breaking.

"Que es?" asked Mardee.

"Es malo con el nino," the boy replied.

"Espera," Mardee ordered. "I'll be back."

Mardee burst into Judge Roberts' office. "There's a boy out here who says his mother is very sick. It sounds like she's having a baby. He wants you to come and help her."

"Go tell Addie to get some clean white rags and come with me," the judge replied as he quickly rose from his desk.

In a matter of minutes the judge and his wife were ready to go on their mission of mercy. As they started out the door Mardee said, "I'll go with you. I can help with the language."

The boy was waiting at the gate, and the tenseness in his face eased as the three emerged.

"Tell him to show us the way," the judge said.

"Donde vive?" Mardee asked.

"Vengan con migo," the boy replied with a smile and a wave of his hand.

Mardee asked the boy a few questions as they hurried down the street. His name was Jorje Gonzales. His mother's name was Anita, and his father's name was Manuel, but he was working on the Luna Ranch at Los Lunas and didn't come home very often. The boy and his mother and his two sisters lived in town. The boy worked in a grocery store cleaning and stocking the shelves to make a few dollars so the family could make ends meet until his father would bring them money.

They soon came to Jorje's home, a two room adobe surrounded by cedar trees. One small window provided the only light as the judge, Addie, Mardee, and Jorje entered. Two little girls ran to meet them. Jorje quickly pointed to his mother on the bed as he took his sisters outside.

"Tell Jorje to build up the fire and put water on the stove," the judge ordered. "Tell the woman we are here to help her," he added looking at her pain-racked face.

Soon the judge and Addie had things progressing smoothly. The woman relaxed somewhat knowing they were there to help her. She knew what to do. She had gone through this three times before. When each pain gripped her body the judge would order, "Empuja, senora, empuja!" as Mardee had told him the Spanish word for push. Addie bathed her forehead with a cool rag and held her hand, softly encouraging her. She didn't speak Spanish, but she spoke the universal language of childbirth.

"You are doing fine Anita," she kept saying as the woman gripped her hands. When the pains deepened the mother's moans became louder, and Mardee stepped outside to be with the boy and his sisters.

"Very soon you will have the new baby," she told Jorje. "Pronto, poco tiempo."

They all sat down near the woodpile, and Mardee started drawing pictures in the loose dirt. The girls were very interested, and as she named the pictures they repeated the English words back to her. They learned several words in a short time: boy, girl, mother, baby, house, wood, sun.

These children had never been to school, Mardee could tell, even though the boy was about fourteen years old, and the girls looked to be about eight and ten. She glanced from the girls' animated faces to the boy's earnest eyes. What a shame, she thought. These children could learn easily. How are they ever going to be able to do anything if they don't get an education?

At that moment Addie opened the door and beckoned to the children. "Baby is here," she said, looking at Mardee. "A perfect little girl!"

"Un nina bella," Mardee announced. "Tu tienes un hermana pequena!"

The little girls squealed with delight at the thought of a baby sister as Jorje grinned with relief.

"Que hermosa," Mardee said softly as she looked at the new baby. Her delicate features were framed with a mass of black hair. One tiny fist flailed the air and then found its way into her rosebud mouth.

"Quieres a comer," the mother whispered and drew the tiny mouth to her breast.

"Thanks for letting me come," Mardee said softly to the judge.

"Thank you," he said, smilingly. "You are a good interpreter. You made it easier for us. I think we can go now."

"Tell the woman we'll bring back food," Addie directed.

"Adios," Mardee said to the woman. "Vamos a nuestra casa y regresamos con comida para ustedes."

As they walked thoughtfully back, Mardee looked up at the judge. "You are both a judge and a doctor!"

Judge Roberts shook his head with a sigh. "Sometimes, out of necessity, but I really prefer the law."

"Why did they call for you?" Mardee asked.

"They ask for me when there is any kind of trouble. It can be when they are sick or when the marshall is after them. They are simple people, Mardee," the judge answered.

"But not if they had some education," Mardee said. "Don't these children go to school? My father makes sure his Spanish workers' children go to school."

The judge shook his head. "I'm afraid not. In fact, many Anglo children do not go to school, either."

I must speak to the governor about this problem, Mardee thought.

Addie had prepared a large pot of beef soup for their supper, so she poured half of it into a bucket for Mardee to take back to the Gonzales family. She also put homemade bread and a squash pie in a small box for them.

Mardee had to make two trips, and the family greeted her with open arms. The baby was now quiet and sleeping, and the mother lay peacefully resting. She opened her eyes when Mardee lightly touched her shoulder. "Yo le llevo caldito para su familia. Como se seinte? You feel all right?" Mardee asked.

"Si, si," the woman replied cheerfully. "Gracias, senorita."

Jorje followed Mardee outside as she was leaving. "Muchas gracias, senorita," he said sincerely and after a moment of hesitation, he asked, "You be my maestra?"

"You want me to teach you?"

"Si," he answered. "Mis numeros en Ingles, por favor."

Mardee looked into the eager young face and her heart went out to him. "Oh yes," she replied. "Vendre aqui manana. I will teach you your numbers."

Jorje's face broke into a broad smile. "Aqui, manana?" He could hardly believe what he had heard.

"Si, si," Mardee assured him as she headed for home to have her own supper.

The next day Mardee settled into a regular routine. She would go home at five o'clock, have her supper, help with the dishes, and then go to the Gonzales home to tutor Jorje for an hour. The little sisters were learning, too. Mardee discovered that she loved to teach, and she enjoyed watching the progress of the new baby.

"Have you decided on a name?" she asked the mother a few days later. "Como se llama ella?"

Mrs. Gonzales smiled shyly. "Esta Esperanza," she replied.

"Esperanza es un nombre muy bello," Mardee assured her. She carefully picked up the pretty child and looked fondly into her somber dark eyes. "Little tiny girl," she crooned softly, "you are our hope. Did you know that, Hope?"

20

Every night when Mardee fell into bed, she read from *Little Women*. Tryouts for the play had been held, and she had been given the role of Jo. She was excited about being in the production, but she was also very nervous.

Fortunately, Mardee's imaginative nature, as well as her sensitivity, helped her play the role. "That girl is amazing," Sister Bernice said to one of the other teachers. "She has the inherent instincts of an actress. It just seems to come naturally."

Meanwhile, the lessons with the Gonzales children were going well. Jorje was learning to add and subtract. He had a talent for numbers. Soon he would be able to handle other tasks at the store besides just cleaning and stocking. He wanted to be able to price merchandise and eventually become a full-fledged clerk handling the cash register.

The little girls were now learning right along with their brother. Mrs. Roberts had loaned Mardee some old McGregor readers her girls had used in the first grade, and the children were all learning to read. Mardee gave them alphabet drill and phonics practice each day and then let them do both oral and silent reading. She had watched Sadie teach reading for many years, so she knew the proper techniques.

The lessons often lasted longer than Mardee planned. If she had any homework she had to do that before getting into bed. She also rose early to help Mrs. Roberts with the morning chores, so her nights were short.

One night as she got into bed it suddenly occured to her that she hadn't thought of Jeff in days. My life is so busy I don't have time to even think about the love of my life, she mused.

One afternoon Mardee went into the governor's office to deliver some letters. "Excuse me, sir, but I have these for you to look over."

"Thank you, Miss Spencer," Governor McDonald replied, smiling. "Sit down a minute. Tell me, how are things going?"

"Oh, they are going very well," Mardee replied. "I hope you are pleased, sir?"

"I am pleased, indeed. John is also pleased. In fact, I hear nothing but good reports about what a great help you are to this office. I want to tell you how much I appreciate your good work."

"Thank you, sir," Mardee replied, blushing.

"And I am writing your father this very day about how you are doing, and I am giving you a good report."

He's so pleased with me; maybe this is a good time to talk to him about schooling for children, Mardee thought. So she smiled and said, "Governor McDonald, I would like to talk to you about something that concerns me."

"Of course, dear. What is it?" he replied.

"You see, sir, I am working with some Spanish children in the evening, teaching them reading and basic arithmetic. I am working with a boy, Jorje, who is fourteen years old, and his younger sisters. These children have never been to school. They are very intelligent, and they are all learning very fast. I think it is so sad that they have never gone to school. There must be many others."

"I'm afraid there are too many just like them," the governor replied.

"But sir, why are these children not going to school?" Mardee asked, a serious expression on her face.

"There probably isn't any one reason," the governor replied. "I know we need more schools and more teachers. The public education program is new in this state. Perhaps part of the problem is apathy and habit. Many parents have never gone to school and don't realize the need for education. I guess the rest of us don't really realize this need, either."

"Can't the state do more to help," Mardee asked.

The governor looked over at this young girl who had worked in his office only a short time. She should be one of my advisors, he thought, instead of some of the worthless ones I have.

"Miss Spencer, you are absolutely right," he said. "I will think about this problem and urge the legislature to act on some new legislation that should help the education problems in our state." He rose and bowed to her. "I'll see what I can do. Thank you for bringing this matter to my attention."

Mardee beamed at the governor. "Governor McDonald, I would also like to extend an invitation to you to attend our play at the school. I know Sister Evangelina and Sister Bernice would be thrilled if you would come."

"What part do you play?" the governor asked with a smile.

"I am Jo in *Little Women*," Mardee said quickly.

"Let me know the time and the day, and Mrs. McDonald and I will be there," he assured her.

Mardee was in a state of euphoria as she walked briskly down the hall toward her office. But happy thoughts were quickly forgotten when she saw a young soldier standing by her door.

Oh no! she thought with exasperation. Stewart Riley.

The young man had regularly come by since Jeff left. So far she had been able to decline his invitations by claiming she was too busy. But he didn't give up easily. "Hello, Stewart," she said brusquely as she breezed past him into her office. Immediately regretting her impatience, she added, "How are you today?"

"Fine," Stewart said eagerly. "I have an idea for us," he added, smiling.

"Oh?" Mardee replied guardedly as she stood behind her desk.

"Yep," the tall, red haired young man with a perennial smile enthusiastically said. "I can borrow two horses for us on Saturday, and we can take a ride into the foothills and pick pinons. How about that?"

I would love to ride a horse again, Mardee thought, and it is about time for the pinon harvest. That would be fun, even with Stewart!

"I do have some time in the afternoon," she replied.

"What time would be convenient?" Stewart asked with a big smile.

"I could leave about one o'clock," Mardee said, "but I should be back by four o'clock. We have play practice on Saturday."

"Just wonderful," Stewart answered happily. "I'll pick you up at one, sharp." He turned briskly and left the room with a sense of victory. He had finally gotten a commitment out of this illusive young woman.

Mardee sat for a moment thinking of the happy days she had spent riding her Gypsy over the Manzano foothills. They seemed a long time ago. Life had gotten much more complicated since she came to Santa Fe. With a big sigh she sat down to continue her afternoon's work. For the first time she missed Jeff. I want to go riding with Jeff, and not with that shiny faced boy, she thought.

The pensive girl looked out her window and caught a glimpse of Stewart talking elatedly with a group of soldiers. Poor me, she thought dourly. And then as an afterthought, poor Stewart, too!

21

That Saturday Mardee lay on the grass under the big elm tree in the front yard reading *Little Women*. In the book Jo had returned home and was dissatisfied and lonely. Mardee knew from the play that Jo would marry the professor, and she wasn't sure she liked that ending. Jo would end up with a disheveled penniless teacher when she could have had handsome rich Laurie. Such is life, she thought as she put the book aside and looked up through the spreading branches. Frost had already come, and richly yellowed leaves were floating lazily down. It was the end of October, and they would perform their play next Friday night.

And where is Jeff? He had been gone a month and not sent her even a note. "Such is life," she repeated outloud, disgustedly, as she noticed Stewart coming down the dirt road on a bay horse and leading a pinto. And her dark mood vanished at the thought of riding again.

She immediately jumped up and waved. "I'll get a jacket and a pail for the pinons," she yelled. "I'll be right back."

Stewart tied the horses to the fence and stood smiling by the pinto, ready to help Mardee mount. She quickly tied the pail on the back of her saddle, and completely ignoring her helpful companion, stepped into the stirrup and lifted herself with ease into the saddle.

"Oh, he's nice!" she exclaimed as she reined him around in circles as Stewart remounted. "What's his name?"

"I call him Spot," Stewart replied with a grin.

"What a dull name!" Mardee retorted with a frown. "You should be Pretty Boy," she said, stroking his neck. "I know, I'll call you Bonito. That's a better name for a handsome fellow like you."

"All right," Stewart said with an easy smile. "Mine is Brownie."

No imagination, Mardee thought to herself. "Who do they belong to?" she asked.

"The Langley Ranch, right out of town. They provide horses for the Cavalry Unit. I had them bring two extra ones in yesterday. They'll leave them here a while to see if we need them in the Cavalry Regiment. We don't right now, so you and I can ride them when we want," Stewart explained proudly.

"How wonderful," Mardee said. "I have missed riding my Gypsy so much. You know, there are times when you just have to ride."

"I know," Stewart said, nodding. "I come from a farm in Illinois, and I always had my horse to ride. That's why I joined the cavalry. And because I'm the only one in the unit who knows anything about horses, I take care of all of them. It's an easy job for me, and I like it."

Mardee couldn't resist any longer. She dug her heels into the horse's sides. "Let's go, Bonito."

The little pinto obeyed her command and dashed off leaving Stewart and his bay behind. For a few moments Mardee imagined herself on her beloved Gypsy riding across the Manzano foothills. At the end of the dirt road where a trail headed toward the mountains, Mardee reined in her spirited mount and waited for Stewart.

"You have a good heart, Bonito," she said with approval, rubbing his sweaty neck. "You are almost as fast as my Gypsy. I think I love you already. Yo te amo, little one," she crooned.

Stewart quickly caught up. "You can ride, girl. Jeff said to get you a good horse because you were a good rider. He was right!"

"Thanks," Mardee said, her voice flat at the mention of Jeff's name.

"Let's ride on a ways," Stewart said. "We will be coming to the pinon trees soon. The pinon nuts should be starting to ripen lower down, so we won't have to go up into the hills too far."

Stewart took off, and this time Mardee let him take the lead. Thoughts of Jeff lingered in her mind. Why wasn't he here riding with her? Because she loved Jeff so much, she had always assumed he felt the same way about her.

Doubts were beginning to form in her mind. Why hadn't she heard from him? If he missed her as much as she missed him, he should be writing her. Her thoughts went back to fiesta night and the rockets bursting in the velvet sky as Jeff held her close and told her he loved her. The memory of the throbbing ecstacy of their kisses caused a dull aching pain of frustration in the pit of her stomach.

Stewart turned his horse toward a clump of pinon trees as Mardee brought her thoughts back to the present. You are not going to spoil this nice day for me, Jeff, she vowed silently. Stewart seems to be a nice fellow. I'm going to enjoy being with him, and you're not going to ruin it, Jeff Corbin!

Mardee now had a smile on her face as the mountain breeze touched her face gently. The Sangre de Cristos rose majestically behind the foothill scrub cedar and pinon trees. "We should find some pinons over here," Stewart yelled back to her. "These look like good trees."

But as they came closer, someone else had gotten there before them. An Indian mother and several little children were picking the pinons off the ground and putting them in one large bucket. "The Indians beat us to them," Stewart said disgustedly. "Heck, those danged Indians!"

"They always pick pinon nuts in the fall," Mardee explained to the midwest boy. "Pinons are a big part of their winter diet."

"The government will give them food. I'm surprised they have the ambition to pick pinons," Stewart said with distaste.

"You don't like Indians very much, do you?" Mardee asked, giving Stewart a sharp look.

"No, do you?" Stewart said emphatically as he turned his horse.

"I have liked all the Indians I have known," Mardee said defensively, "but I haven't known many Indians." Then she asked, "Have you?"

"I guess I haven't, really," Stewart answered, "but I've had to fight quite a few. When they get on the warpath and are full of whiskey they aren't very likeable, I know that."

Mardee thought about what the young soldier had said and realized that he had his reasons. Then she sadly thought, He probably won't like me when he knows I'm part Indian.

"Here's a good place," Stewart said, pointing. "Let's try our luck."

They climbed off their horses, tied them to the branches of a cedar tree, and took a look. "Get your bucket," Stewart said. "There is a good crop here. We'll beat the Indians and squirrels to them."

Pinon trees only bear their prize crop once every seven years. So there may be one tree with many nuts right next to one with none. Fortunately, several of the trees in this clump were bearing this year. When they had gathered all the nuts on the ground, they shook more from the trees.

They moved from tree to tree and the afternoon passed pleasantly as they filled their pail and talked. Pinon nuts are so small it takes many, many nuts to fill even a small pail, but with both of them picking, the container was soon half full. "Let's rest a while," Mardee said. "Mrs. Roberts sent some ginger cookies for us."

The two young people then sat under one of the trees, and Mardee found Stewart easy to talk to. She was genuinely interested in the Army stories he told her. "You must love being in the Army," Mardee said. "I'm sure it is much more interesting than being on a farm in Illinois."

"Yes," he agreed, "but I miss the farm and my family. I would like to see my dad and my mother and little sister, Polly." Stewart's face became thoughtful for a moment. Then he smiled and looked over at Mardee. "Polly is about your age, but she has long blonde pigtails."

"I'll bet she misses you, too," Mardee said. "I know I miss my brothers, especially my little brother, Roy. He's so cute with bright blue eyes and a square little chin. He's the youngest of the four boys, but the most determined."

Stewart then told Mardee about Illinois farm life, and she described life on the Manzano ranch and explained about the sawmill. His family raised corn; hers raised beans. His family raised hogs; her family raised cattle. Both were pleased to have an interested listener.

I like him afterall, Mardee thought. I wish I had an older brother like him. She was aware of the comfortable rapport between them.

Suddenly Stewart looked up at the sun. "The afternoon is half gone," he said, jumping up. "We'd better get busy and fill this pail. Come on, lazy girl."

They soon found a clump of trees laden with pinons and had their pail full in an hour. "I'm thirsty," Stewart said as they neared the outskirts of town. "Let's go to the mercantile and get ourselves a cold drink."

"Wonderful!" Mardee said, anticipating a cold root beer.

They quickly tied their horses at the rail and went inside. Stewart selected their drinks from an ice barrel as Mardee went down the aisle to greet Jorje.

"So you are stocking shelves today. Are you putting the prices on the cans, too?"

Jorje smiled and pointed to the cans of beans. "Yes, today I do it. See?"

"I'm so proud of you!" Mardee exclaimed.

Jorje didn't understand everything Mardee said, but he knew she was pleased, and that made him happy. "Yes, Mardee," he said. "Hoy mi trabajo es bueno. My job is good."

Mardee then gave him a quick hug and went to join Stewart who was paying for the drinks. They sat on a bench outside the store, savoring the cold liquid without talking. As she took the last swallow Mardee said, "Thank you for a wonderful day, Stewart. I have enjoyed it so much."

"Thank you," Stewart said smiling. "I enjoyed it, too. We must do it again."

"I can walk to play practice from here," Mardee said, getting up stiffly. "I can certainly tell I haven't ridden a horse for a while." She slowly straightened up. "You take the pinons. You can bring some to me tomorrow," she said as she walked over to the pinto. "Goodbye, little Bonito. Thank you for the nice ride. Stewart will give you some good oats and a long drink of cold water soon because you are such a good boy." She gave the pony a hug and brushed his muzzle with a soft kiss. Then with a happy wave she was off.

I really did enjoy the day, she thought as she walked along.

The only unpleasant thing had been Stewart's attitude toward Indians. It made her uncomfortable, and she knew they must discuss this more fully at a later time. She smiled to herself. You are thinking of seeing Stewart again, aren't you? Then she chided herself. You gave him a chance, and he turned out to be a nice fellow, didn't he? Did you learn something today, Mardeegirl? I think so!

22

The next week was a chaotic mix of play practices, dress rehearsals, nerves, and tears. Learning the lines to perfection and pleasing the almost unpleasable Sister Bernice was really a challenge. Mardee's natural talent and ability to memorize long passages served her well in rehearsal, but sometimes her interpretation of the part did not agree with what the director wanted. And Sister Bernice was more strong minded than Mardee. When Mardee's character, Jo, came home with a dollar for having sold her first story, Mardee played the scene as an ecstatic young girl who broke into tears at this initial writing success. But Sister Bernice had no patience with the tears. "You have just sold your first story, Mardee," she said impatiently. "You are happy. You don't cry when you are happy."

"Sometimes I do," Mardee said quietly.

"Well, you shouldn't," Sister Bernice instructed in a determined voice. "When you are happy you laugh, not cry." And that settled the question. So Mardee rejoiced over Jo's sale outwardly on the stage, but inwardly she was choking back the tears as she thought of Jo's accomplishment. At any rate, Mardee knew Jo's courage would always be an inspiration to her, and her struggle to control her inward emotion on stage resulted in the powerful performance Sister Bernice was hoping to bring out.

Mrs. Roberts had gone through her trunks and found clothes that would be suitable for the Civil War Era. Mardee had long full skirts and high necked blouses to wear, along with wide brimmed hats and high topped shoes with spindly high heels. Mardee felt very elegant as she pranced around the stage, spinning on her heels and swirling her skirts. She wore her hair long and natural as Jo did, but when Jo cut her hair and sold it in the story she had to conceal her abundant curls in a tight flattened roll.

Mardee almost wished she had gotten one of the male roles. She thought it would be fun to dress up like a boy and wear trousers and straw hats and bow ties. And it would be very daring to wear pants instead of skirts, Mardee thought.

Nevertheless, I'm Jo, Mardee told herself as she prepared for the dress rehearsal on Thursday afternoon. And I don't think I'll ever get all my lines right. And that won't please Sister Bernice.

The dress rehearsal went well, even if Sister Bernice still looked somewhat dissatisfied. But the teacher knew that the first stage fright was over now, and the night performance would go better. After she dismissed the cast and sent them home to relax before the next show, she gave Mardee a hug and whispered in her ear that she had done well. "I'll do better tonight, I promise," she said, her confidence returning.

Sister Bernice smiled a rare smile as Mardee headed for home.

Shortly, as Mardee walked past the judge's office downstairs, she could not believe her eyes when she spotted a familiar figure staring back at her. "Papa!" she screamed as she ran into his arms. "What are you doing here?"

"I'm here for your play, of course," he replied as he extracted himself from her arms. "Let me stand up, dear, so I can look at you properly."

"Oh Papa, I'm so thrilled you're here!"

"I'm happy, too," he assured her. "You know I wouldn't miss a play. There, there, don't cry. You'll mess up that pretty face." He took out his big handkerchief and gently wiped her cheeks. "What's this?" he asked in mock indignation as he noticed the red stains on his handkerchief. "Rouge on my daughter? I'll have to speak to Sister Evangelina about this."

"Oh Papa," she said quickly, "it's only stage makeup." Then looking at him coyly, she added, "All we great actresses have to wear it."

"Sorry to interrupt," Mrs. Roberts said, "but Mardee, you must eat a light snack and then bathe and rest a while before the performance." She then took Mardee's hand. "We'll have a little get-together after the show here at the house, and you two will have lots of time to talk then."

Mardee blew a kiss to her father. Now everything will be all right, she thought happily to herself.

23

Such rapport with the audience, Sister Bernice marveled silently as Mardee played the part of Jo to perfection. She has an amazing insight into human actions and reactions for one so young, she smilingly thought.

At the end of the play the whole cast took bows to two standing ovations, and after the curtains were finally drawn Sister Evangelina made her way to the front of the auditorium. She thanked the cast and its director, Sister Bernice. Then she thanked all the parents and visitors, especially Ben Spencer who had come so far for the evening's performance. Then she introduced Governor McDonald and his wife who stood and received a loud round of applause.

"Would you favor us with a few words?" Sister Evangelina asked.

The governor smiled broadly as he came forward. He praised the performances and gave a special thanks to Mardee Spencer from his own office. He spoke a few words about the Loretta Academy.

"This school for girls has been functioning since 1853 when the Sisters of Loretta founded it," he began. "Because of these wonderful nuns, our girls in New Mexico receive educations comparable to those in the eastern schools. This educational institution is a model for education, and I will be consulting with Sister Evangelina as I prepare my educational program for the new state of New Mexico. With her help next year, I will be able to present to the Legislature my plans for an outstanding education system for the entire state. Thank you, Sisters of Loretta, for all you have done for our girls and for education in the state."

Governor McDonald then took Sister Evangelina's hand and bowed graciously. Sister smiled, thanked him, and turned to the audience as she invited them to visit with the actors before leaving.

Suddenly, as Mardee looked over the crowd, a tall redhead emerged, walking right in her direction. He does look kind of handsome in his uniform, Mardee was forced to admit to herself as Stewart Riley gave her a hug. When she introduced him to her father and Judge Roberts and Mrs. Roberts, Ben gave him a sharp look and then beamed. He liked what he saw.

Raquel Sanchez, one of Mardee's actress friends at the school, and her family were now pushing their way through the crowd. The two girls hugged each other as if they had been separated for a long time, and Mardee proudly presented Raquel and her parents to the group.

"Good performance," the governor said as he bowed over Raquel's hand. "You played the part of the mother with wonderful feeling."

A familiar voice caught Mardee's attention above the babble of conversations. "Como esta, mi estrella?" Turning around, she looked up to find a tall dark haired man grinning down at her in amusement. "How's my little star?" he repeated in English. "Hello, Mardita. Why do you always forget me, mi hita?"

"Frankie?" she asked in wonderment, "Is it really you?"

"Of course," he said with a soft laugh. "It's good to see you, querida." He put his arms around her, and suddenly he was friend, home, and security all mixed together. How she had missed him!

Finally, she eased back and looked closely at his familiar face. He appeared older and his dark eyes less merry than she remembered.

"How did you get here?" she asked.

"I came with your father," he answered. "We'll explain it all later."

Just then Addie Roberts addressed the group. "You are all invited to our house for a reception for our fine little actresses, Mardee and Raquel. Governor and Mrs. McDonald are coming, so let's all be on our way. They can't stay too long."

The governor and the judge were still busy talking with some of the crowd, so Mrs. Roberts turned to Mardee and said, "Let's go on ahead and get the food set out."

"I'll go with you," Raquel offered.

Stewart and Frankie quickly joined the girls and they all walked the short distance together. They soon had the dining room table laden with cold beverages, cookies, and candies.

Ben Spencer and the Sanchezes and the governor's wife arrived shortly, escorting Sister Evangelina and Sister Bernice. The governor and the judge followed closely behind.

The judge opened a bottle of champagne that had been cooling in a bucket of ice, served everyone, and then raised his glass for a round of toasts. Mardee and Raquel and Sister Bernice received one for their wonderful play, as did Sister Evangelina for the wonderful school. The governor and his wife were next for their wonderful leadership, and then the parents of the actresses, and finally one to all the other guests. Governor McDonald proposed the last toast, "To the wonderful state of New Mexico and the hope we have for the future."

Mardee looked around at all the happy faces and thought, I wish this night would last forever. I think I will never be so happy again.

As people broke into small groups Mardee led Frankie out to the front porch, and they sat in the swing while they sipped their drinks. "I've never had champagne before," Mardee said. "Mother Spencer would die if she saw me now!"

Frankie looked at Mardee with discerning eyes. "You seem very happy, Mardita. Things must be going well for you."

"I am happy now," Mardee said, "because you and Papa are here."

"We're both happy to be here," Frankie said solemnly.

"You said you had some things to tell me?" Mardee asked.

"Yes," Frankie said, looking thoughtfully in the distance. "Your father and I are here on railroad business. I am now a railroad detective, and I will be here for a few weeks to attend law enforcement classes. Your father has been made a special deputy to work on a case in the mountain area, so he has come here to meet with Santa Fe Railroad officials to be briefed on the case. He will be here only a couple of days."

"You two drove up together, then?" Mardee asked.

"Yes, Ben came to Belen and picked me up," Frankie replied.

Mardee was surprised at the thought of her father and Frankie together. "Did you have a nice trip?" she questioned curiously.

"Sure," Frankie replied. "We had a little trouble getting up Lavahara Hill. The car kept heating up. But otherwise, that's a pretty good road between here and Albuquerque."

"How's your father?" Mardee asked, not knowing what to say next.

"He's fine," Frankie said, "but lonely, of course." Placing a finger under Mardee's chin and tipping up her face, he added, "And so am I. Lonely, I mean. How about you, Mardita?"

"Oh, I've missed everyone," Mardee answered quickly, "but I am enjoying my life here." Then jumping down from the swing, she said brightly, "Let's go in the house and visit with the others. You and I will have lots of time to catch up later. Come on in, and I'll introduce you to the Sanchezes. They are very nice people, and you will enjoy Raquel."

Mardee introduced Frankie and excused herself as she joined the governor's group.

"I'm so glad you invited me," Governor McDonald said. "I enjoyed the evening very much, and your talents never cease to amaze me." He turned to Ben. "She types, she writes letters in either English or Spanish, she interprets, she teaches English to Spanish children, she's a good student, and now she proves to be a wonderful actress. What an outstanding daughter you have!"

"Thank you, Governor," Ben replied with a smile. "She gets it all from me, you know!"

"Well, not her looks," the governor replied with a wink.

"I'll agree with you there, sir," Ben said, laughing.

The governor then pulled his gold watch out of his pocket. "I have stayed longer than I meant to, but this is such a pleasant party I let time get away from me." Turning to his wife he said, "We must go, my dear. Let us say our goodbyes to our hosts. Ben, it was so good seeing you again."

Judge Roberts and Addie had been excellent hosts, but Governor

McDonald and his wife's departure was the signal for everyone to say goodnight. Mardee kissed her father and assured Frankie that she would look forward to seeing him very soon.

She then thanked Stewart for coming and suggested they ride together next weekend. As she walked Raquel and her parents and the two nuns to the front gate, she gave Sister Evangelina and Sister Bernice big hugs.

Happily returning to the house, Mardee helped Mrs. Roberts clear the table and put things away. "I can never thank you enough for all you do for me, Mrs. Roberts," she said as she put her arms around her. "Thank you for the wonderful party. I will remember this night for the rest of my life. You made everything perfect. Thank you, again, so much."

"You are very welcome, my dear," Mrs. Roberts said. "I enjoy doing things for you." She then gave Mardee a kiss on the cheek. "Go to bed, little girl. We'll talk about all this tomorrow. You really were quite the star tonight, you know!"

24

Ben completed his briefings with the Santa Fe Railroad officials, and he and Mardee had breakfast together on Sunday before he left. After a hearty meal of sausage, eggs, and hot cakes at his hotel, Ben then asked for a second cup of coffee as he sat enjoying his daughter's company. "Well, school and the job seem to be going very well. How is Jeff these days? I understand he is out of town."

"Yes," Mardee said, unable to hide her exasperation. "He has been gone over a month, and I have not heard a word from him. Papa, I don't think I understand what is going on. I know he cares for me, but I think he is trying to avoid me."

As the waitress set Ben's steaming coffee in front of him, he raised it and blew on it a few seconds before replying. "Mardee, I told you before not to get too emotionally involved with Jeff," he said slowly. "His career comes first with him. The governor tells me he is being considered for an appointment in the legal department in Washington, D.C. He will probably get that appointment, and deservedly so."

Ben paused for a few moments as he sipped the hot coffee. "Jeff is fond of you, Mardee, but don't build up any hopes for anything serious between you and him. His career comes first. It's that simple."

Mardee stared into her father's eyes. "What are you saying, Papa? Do you know something I don't?"

Ben reached for his daughter's hand. "Darlin', I'm just saying that Jeff is a man with a bright future, and that future may not include you. You have to be prepared for that." Ben then patted his daughter's hand.

"Well," Mardee said defensively, "Jeff isn't the only man in the world.

Stewart Riley is a very nice boy, and now that Frankie is here I'll be seeing him, too."

"Yes, seeing Stewart is fine," her father agreed. "And I'm sure Frankie will be around. But he's going to be pretty busy, so he may not have much time for you. He will be taking some difficult law enforcement courses. This is a serious case we're working on, and he needs to know what he is doing. He can't afford to make any mistakes."

"Tell me about the family," she said brightly, wanting to change the subject. "What are Mother Spencer and the boys doing?"

"The same old things," Ben answered with a smile. "Sadie is busy, as always, with the school and the post office. Lola is helping her with the housework and doing a good job. She's learning to make bread that's almost better than yours," he said teasingly. "The boys are growing up," he added quietly.

Talking about the family made Mardee homesick. "Can I come home for Christmas, Papa?" she asked.

"Sure," he said easily. "You can take the train down to Mountainair, and I'll pick you up."

At the thoughts of a train ride and going home, the sparkle in Mardee's eyes returned. For the moment, thoughts of Jeff were left behind.

Ben quickly finished his coffee. "Come on, dear," he said briskly. "I've got to get you back to the Robertses and head down the road. I need to be at the mill tomorrow to check on some orders." As he paid for breakfast he took a twenty dollar bill out of his wallet and handed it to Mardee. "That's for your train fare," he said smiling. "There are going to be some pleased boys when they hear you are coming home."

25

Mardee pulled her winter coat tightly around her waist and buttoned it up to her throat as she left the Governor's Palace. She tied a woolen scarf around her head and took a deep breath of the crisp November air. The soft snowflakes warned of the winter which would soon come in earnest.

These were good times for Mardee. She was still basking in the glow of her acting success, and Sister Bernice had insisted that she learn to sing. She looked forward now to Wednesdays when she would climb into the choir loft and join the others, and she was becoming one of the leaders at school even though she was only a part-time student.

Meanwhile, to emphasize her concern about the lack of education in the state, she had brought her students, Lucy and Dora, to the governor's office so they could show what they had learned in only two months. She hoped that by the first of the year she could talk their mother into sending the two girls to school. "By then," she told Governor McDonald, "the girls should be able to go into the second grade and keep up with the rest of the students."

The two little dark eyed girls had made her point about education. The governor had asked Mardee to write to the Education Department in Washington to determine the United States National Education Policy.

In a short time Mardee received an answer assuring her that education was of major interest. "We are constantly examining how education is organized, structured, delivered, and assessed in order to improve quality, ensure equal access for all, and make education activities better serve the needs of our country," the letter stated.

Mardee underlined the words, "ensure equal access for all" when she presented the letter to Governor McDonald. In the margin she wrote, "This is our problem. Our state must put ALL our children in school even if parents are unaware of the need for it."

The letter also explained that there was no national law on education in the United States; no federal guarantee of a right to education exists; this is left up to the individual states. Although the rights and privileges of students are determined by federal law and Constitutional law pertaining to citizens' rights, state laws are the ones that determine the education policies for the state's citizens. Mardee added another note at the end of this paragraph: "Therefore, the need for New Mexico to review its present education laws and legislate new laws that will improve education."

Mardee had also gone back to 1774 to 1779 and researched educational statements made by the Continental Congress and the Constitutional Convention, and she gave these quotes to Governor McDonald: "Schools, and the means of education, shall be encouraged," and "The utmost good faith shall always be observed towards the Indians." Her terse comment at the end of these statements was, "New Mexico is not doing this, for shame."

Mardee's next assignment was writing to the surrounding states asking for information on their educational policy. "We will give all this information to Jeff when he gets back," the governor said, "and he can go from there in determining what laws we need to present to the Legislature when it meets in January. I definitely think we need a law that mandates school attendance until the age of sixteen."

Mardee was excited to be involved in this project. Her interest stemmed from the fact that education had been a high priority in her family. Ben made sure all the children went to school, and Sadie made sure they learned. Mardee realized how fortunate she had been to be a part of such a family.

So school and work are going well, Mardee thought as she hurried home. And having Frankie here, even though I don't see him very often, is comforting. He's becoming so serious, though, she thought as she frowned. All he thinks about are his law courses and his work.

Mardee had never asked any details about the case Frankie and her father were working on, but it wasn't from lack of curiousity. For some reason, she always felt a puzzling anxiety when she thought about it.

Mardee's thoughts were suddenly interrupted as Stewart caught up with her. "Can I walk with you a ways?" he asked, smiling. "I need to talk to you."

"Certainly," Mardee said, "what do you want to talk about?"

"I want to talk about, well, I want to talk about Raquel," Stewart blurted out.

"What about her?" Mardee asked, covering a smile. Raquel had talked about Stewart ever since the night of the play.

"Well, I thought she was a nice girl, and pretty, too. But she's Mexican, isn't she?"

"She's Spanish," Mardee corrected. "Her parents have a ranch at Cienega, which is part of a land grant from the King of Spain. Her ancestors came directly from Spain. The Mexicans come from Mexico, and many are mixed with Indians. But Raquel is Spanish."

"Oh," Stewart said breathing a sigh of relief. "So she has no Indian blood?"

"No, but what if she did?" Mardee asked sharply. "And since you don't like Indians, you'd just better walk right back to the post. You happen to be with one of them right now."

Mardee abruptly stopped in her tracks and faced Stewart with hands on her hips. Her cheeks were bright red from anger rising inside her. "And one more thing," she spat out. "Don't say anything else about Mexicans, either. The best friend I have in the world is part Mexican. Don't be so stupid, Stewart. And don't talk to me again until you can make more sense."

With that, Mardee whirled around and headed for home, leaving a surprised and confused soldier standing there wiping his brow.

As Mardee burst into the front hall she stamped her feet in exasperation, frightening a Mexican woman who was dusting the wall lamps. Not meaning to scare the cleaning lady, she gave her a weak smile and murmured, "No es nada. Perdon, por favor. I'm sorry."

As she passed the judge's office he motioned her in. "Who is she?"

Mardee asked, pointing toward the hall.

"Remember Martin who was in my office a few days ago insisting that I sue his wife because she had burned up his money?" the judge asked with a grin.

"Oh yes," Mardee said, as she thought back. Martin had been working on a ranch and had come home with two crisp ten dollar bills. His wife was not at home, and he thought she was probably visiting her mother in Glorieta, so he decided to go down to the tavern and celebrate. However, he didn't want to spend all his hard earned money in the bar, so he put one of the ten dollar bills in his pocket, and thought he would leave one bill at home. But he wanted to hide the money, so he settled on a place where he was sure no one would find it--in the stove since the fire was long out. He shook down the ashes, put some wood on the grate, and stuck the ten dollar bill between two pieces of wood.

When Martin returned home in the early hours of the morning, he was alarmed to see smoke curling out of his chimney. His wife had come home, built a fire to warm up the cold house, and crawled into bed.

Martin had been very upset with his wife for burning up his money, and he had come to the judge. He wanted his wife sued and made to pay back the money. It didn't matter that she had no money. In fact, the only money she ever had was what he gave her. But he felt the judge should figure out a way to punish his wife. "She must be taught a lesson," he had said. "Ensena un leccion a ella."

Judge Roberts was known as a fair man, and Martin felt sure he would right this wrong for him. "Did you ever think that you would have both of your ten dollar bills if you had stayed home that night, Martin?" Judge Roberts pointed out to the complaining husband.

"No, my wife, she burn up the money, so I have no money," he corrected the judge.

"Finally, I figured out what to do," Judge Roberts said as Mardee listened, fascinated. Martin's wife will work for Addie doing whatever cleaning she needs until she earns the ten dollars. That will probably be about a month, so eventually, Martin will have his money back, and his wife will have the esteem of her husband back. Don't you think that's a good solution?"

"I guess so," Mardee replied slowly. "I guess it is good for everyone but the wife. She has to do all the work."

"Oh, she will be happy, too, because Addie will give her food when she is here, as well as some extra clothes she has gathering dust in the closet. She also has a beautiful mantilla she will give her as a special present when she is finished. Now what do you think?"

"You're very clever," Mardee declared as she patted his broad shoulder. "I'll know who to come to when I have unsolvable problems." Like narrow-minded soldiers who don't know what they are talking about, she thought.

26

"It's the storm before Thanksgiving," Mardee thought as she left the Academy on her way to the Governors Palace. She quickened her steps while the cold wind and snow swirled around her. Papa always said to look for a bad storm around Thanksgiving, she reminded herself.

Mardee pulled the heavy door open with difficulty as the wind blew hard against it and stamped her feet on the rug inside the room. John Weeks looked up. "Look what the wind blew in," he said with a grin.

"I'm glad to be in and not out," she said as she approached his desk. "What do you have for me today?"

"There are some letters on your desk. Also, be at the governor's office at two o'clock. He'll need you to help with a guest. Oh, by the way, Jeff Corbin is back. He's in his office."

"Jeff is back," she repeated to herself breathlessly as she hurried to her office. I'll just get out of my coat, she thought. Mardee shivered from the cold as she turned around to start down the hall to Jeff's office and was surprised to find Stewart blocking her door.

Stewart's young face was very serious as he said quickly, "Mardee, I'm sorry for what I said yesterday. Please forgive me."

Mardee, still thinking about Jeff, didn't know what he was talking about for a moment. Then she suddenly remembered their conversation about Indians. Instantly the anger flooded back, and she tossed her head defiantly as she faced him. "Stewart, I am part Indian, and I don't like the feelings you have about Indians."

"I didn't know, Mardee. You don't look like an Indian. I mean, well, you just don't look Indian."

"It doesn't matter how I look on the outside," Mardee answered sharply. "There is Indian blood flowing through the inside. My mother was part Cherokee Indian."

"I . . . I'm sorry," Stewart replied lamely.

"Don't be sorry," Mardee retorted. "I'm not."

"I mean, well, maybe I was wrong. There's certainly nothing wrong with you," Stewart said quickly. His face was very red, even redder than usual.

Mardee could never stay mad at anyone for any length of time. She walked over and put her hand on his arm. "Stewart, you are not totally wrong; you have your reasons for the way you feel. But just remember, never make blanket statements about people. Some are good, some are bad, no matter what race they belong to." She looked earnestly up into his uncomfortable eyes.

"Of course, you're right, Mardee," Stewart said. "I guess I have just never really thought about it that much."

"Well, think about it," Mardee suggested. "By the way," she said brightly, " you have an invitation to the Sanchez Ranch for Thanksgiving dinner. That's something else you can think about. They are Spanish people, you know." Mardee smiled teasingly up at the red-faced soldier.

"Oh Mardee, that would be wonderful!"

"Then I'll tell them you accept?" Mardee asked with a smile.

"Of course," Stewart declared. "I wouldn't pass up a chance to be with Raquel, would I?"

"And Stewart," Mardee said as he turned to leave, "thanks for the apology. I really don't want to lose you as a very good friend."

Mardee then collected her thoughts. Her heart was pounding now at the thought of seeing Jeff again. She felt that he hadn't treated her very well, so she decided not to let him know how much she had missed him as she knocked lightly on his door.

Jeff sat at his desk with a thoughtful frown on his face. The sun from his window shone golden on his hair as his blue eyes lifted to meet Mardee's gaze. She felt a wave of adoration spread over her body, and she only wanted to fall into his arms. Instead, "Hello, Jeff," in a small voice was all she could muster.

"Hello, Mardee," he said with enthusiasm as he rose from his desk and came around to greet her. He lightly kissed her hand, but as she instinctively moved closer he stepped quickly back and smilingly said, "It's so good to see you. How have you been?"

"Fine," Mardee said, gathering her wits. "Just fine. I have missed you."

"But I hear Stewart took good care of you," Jeff said teasingly.

"Stewart and I are friends," Mardee said firmly. "But I missed you." She waited for him to say the same.

"You know, Mardee, I am very busy today. My work here has suffered while I've been gone. I do want to see you and talk to you. Would it be all right if I come by your house tonight after supper?" Jeff looked into Mardee's face intently.

"Of course," Mardee said. "I don't have time to talk now, either." She forced herself to leave, reluctantly.

"See you tonight," Jeff called out as she made her retreat.

Mardee's heart was still pounding, but now it was from anger. He goes away for weeks and doesn't even send me a card. Now he's too busy to talk to me. Well, Jeff Corbin, if that's the way you want it, that's fine with me, Mardee thought as she flounced back to her office.

That evening Mardee decided to talk to Mrs. Roberts about her situation with Jeff. She instinctively knew there were complications she didn't understand. Feeling as close as she did to the older woman, she felt she needed her counsel.

"Mrs. Roberts," she said, as she took dishes down from the cabinet to set the table, "Jeff Corbin is back, and I don't think he wanted to see me today. Why do you suppose that is?"

When Mrs. Roberts didn't answer, Mardee turned around and looked at her questioningly.

"I don't understand the way he acted today," Mardee went on. "Do you suppose there is something wrong?"

Mrs. Roberts followed Mardee to the table. "Put the dishes down, dear, and sit down a minute," she said gently. "I'm going to be honest with you, my dear, because I think you deserve honesty."

"What is it?" Mardee asked anxiously. "Is Jeff involved with someone else?"

Mrs. Roberts slowly nodded her head. "The talk is that he and Heather Dunlap are engaged and will be married in the spring. I'm sorry, but that is what I hear," Mrs. Roberts said, holding Mardee's hands.

"Who is Heather Dunlap?" Mardee asked in a dull voice.

"She's the lieutenant governor's daughter. She's been in school in Virginia, but will finish at Christmas time. Jeff has been in Washington, as you know. I guess they got together when he was back there," Mrs. Roberts explained.

Mardee's heart turned cold like the icy wind outside. I'm not going to cry, she told herself firmly. I'll never cry over him again. As Mrs. Roberts looked at her compassionately she said, "Thank you for telling me. I guess I should have known."

Mrs. Roberts had expected an emotional outburst. "Mardee, I'm so proud of you, "she said with relief. "You're not going to let this throw you, I hope."

"Well, it certainly doesn't make me feel good," Mardee said dryly. "But I'm not going to let him know how bad I feel. Have I been terribly naive, Mrs. Roberts?"

"You are young, Mardee, and you are very open and honest with your feelings. This will hurt, but you have learned from this situation. You are smart, and you won't let it happen again. I'm so sorry, dear," she said as she drew the girl into her arms.

I'm not going to cry, Mardee repeated to herself.

Mardee had just finished with the dishes when Jeff knocked on the door. "I'll get it," she said, grabbing her wrap. She stepped outside and led Jeff over to the porch swing.

The two young people sat in silence for a moment, and then Jeff cleared his throat. "Mardee, I have something to tell you. I don't want you to hear it from anyone else." He paused and looked into her expressionless face. "You have been very special to me, Mardee, and I imagine you always will be. But I have made a decision to marry a girl whom I have known for some time. There will be an engagement announcement in the paper next week. We will be married in the spring."

Mardee's heart almost stopped, but she wanted to say something mature even though she only felt like dying. "Congratulations, Jeff," she heard herself say. "I guess I knew something was not right with us when you didn't write me."

"I'm sorry," he said sincerely.

Mardee looked straight into his eyes. "But Jeff, you said you loved me. Why did you say that if it wasn't true?"

Jeff looked deeply into her wounded eyes. "Mardee, I said I loved you and I did. It just wasn't meant to be, but don't ever doubt my love for you."

Mardee felt only hurt and confusion now as she quickly got up and put out her hand. "Goodnight, Jeff," she said in a choking voice.

"Goodbye, Mardee," Jeff said as he held her hand tightly, brushing it with his lips. "Don't ever forget," he whispered hoarsely. "I loved you very much. Don't ever doubt that, little girl from the mountains."

Mardee jerked her hand away and rushed into the house. She went blindly down the hall, past the judge's office, past the kitchen, and up the stairs. She paused at the top and walked to the window overlooking the front yard.

Jeff was just going through the gate. He walked slowly, his hands in his coat pockets, his head down. "I'm not going to cry," she mumbled. "I'm not going to cry, Jeff Corbin. And thanks to you, I'll never be a sweet vulnerable girl again. You have taught me to protect my heart from now on."

27

Addie Roberts was just placing a bowl of scrambled eggs on the table as Mardee came into the kitchen. "Good morning, sweetie," she said, her sharp eyes noticing the pale face and slightly dulled eyes. "How are you?"

"I'm fine," Mardee said with a sigh as she sat down. "I'm not very hungry, though."

"You don't have to be hungry to eat these buttermilk pancakes," Mrs. Roberts assured her. "They'll melt in your mouth." The two golden brown creations in Mardee's plate demanded attention. "Here's the maple syrup, and the butter is fresh from yesterday. We'll have our breakfast together. The judge is already tending to business in his office."

The quiet girl and the concerned woman ate in silence for a few minutes. Finally, Mardee raised her eyes. "Why does everyone I love leave me, Mrs. Roberts? What's wrong with me?"

"Mardee, let's think about what's right with you," Mrs. Roberts responded, "because there is so much more right than wrong. You are young and pretty and smart and talented, and you have one of the sweetest hearts that God ever put into a person."

"But everyone leaves me," Mardee continued in a lifeless tone. "My mother didn't stay with me. My grandmother died, and now Jeff is gone. Why?"

Mrs. Roberts spoke slowly as she organized her thoughts and words. "Mardee, your grandmother died because her body could not go on physically. She did not want to leave you, I'm sure. I know she must have loved you more than anybody in the world. But when God decides he needs us with him, we must do what he wants. He probably had a big job in Heaven that only your grandmother could help him do. But don't think she isn't still watching over you all the time. Think back later to some things that have almost happened to you, but didn't. That's because your grandmother is watching over you with her everloving eyes. She had to leave you, but she will never stop loving you." Mrs. Roberts paused. "Do you understand what I am saying, Mardee?"

Mardee looked into the firm gaze of Addie Roberts. "Yes, I do know you are right. My grandmother said she would always be with me, and I'm sure she is."

"All right," Mrs. Roberts continued. "Now your mother must have been a very troubled unhappy young woman. We don't know what made her so sad that she would leave her baby, but there was something very wrong. But it wasn't with you. Weren't you better off with your father and your grandmother than you would have been with your mother and the man she left with?" Mardee thought back to what she had heard regarding the man with whom her mother had eloped. They had always been in financial trouble, and she knew her father had helped them many times.

"Yes," Mardee said thoughtfully, "I'm sure I was better off with my father and grandmother. I have never thought of it quite that way before. I certainly am glad I was not taken away from the two people who have meant the most to me."

"Then don't blame yourself for your mother's leaving," Mrs. Roberts said. "Her reasons lay between your father and herself. No one knows those reasons but the two of them. You did not cause her to leave. She probably stayed longer than she wanted to because of you. Never doubt that your mother loved you," Mrs. Roberts finished forcefully.

A faint smile came over Mardee's face. "I'm so lucky to have you, Mrs. Roberts," she said in a more hopeful voice. "But what about Jeff? Why have I lost Jeff?"

Mrs. Roberts took a deep breath. "Well, I'm not sure I have the answers there," she said hesitantly. "Jeff wasn't totally honest with you, I think, because he didn't tell you about the other girl. But I can understand that, too. You are such a desirable young thing that you could sweep any man off his feet. I think Jeff was intrigued with you, and he probably did fall in love with you. But in the long run he realized that he wanted to make his life with the other girl. I don't really know why he made that decision. But I do know," she continued quickly, "he's probably going to be sorry for it one day. He may be feeling as bad as you are right now, Mardee."

"I hope he does," Mardee's words shot out with a spark of her old fire. "I'll never let another man make such a fool of me."

"Yes, you are a wiser girl this morning, Mardee," Mrs. Roberts agreed. "All of us girls have stories like this to tell. Sometime I'll tell you about the cowboy who loved and left me," she finished with a smile.

"Oh really? I'm sorry," Mardee said.

"Nothing to be sorry about," Mrs. Roberts said merrily. "I wouldn't trade my judge for all the cowboys in New Mexico! Now finish your hotcakes, my dear. You've got a busy day ahead of you."

Mardee felt better, but she told herself she would never get over losing Jeff. He is my one and only love, she thought dramatically.

As Mardee walked through the crisp coldness of the morning on her way to school, the mountain air rejuvenated her emotion tossed body. "I will lift up mine eyes to the hills," she said to herself, "from whence cometh my help." She breathed in the clean fresh air deeply and knew that she would survive this heartache.

Mardee worked hard at her lessons that day, but her teachers noticed that her usual smile was missing. She's maturing into a serious young woman, Sister Bernice said to herself.

Mardee approached her work that afternoon with the same total dedication. Jeff stopped by her office briefly and complimented her efforts on the education project. "I'm working on the bill we will present to the Legislature which will ask for more funding for education as well as a law which will mandate school attendance by all children in New Mexico until the age of sixteen," he said seriously.

"That sounds very good," Mardee replied cooly. "I will feel much better knowing that the children of New Mexico are going to be able to have good educations." As she returned to her work she thought, You'll never know how much you hurt me, Jeff.

"I'll show you the bills when I have finished, and we'll probably want you to testify before the Education Committee later," Jeff continued hurriedly.

"Of course," Mardee responded coldly. "Now if you will excuse me, I'm very busy."

Mardee glanced up in time to notice Jeff's red face as he turned to leave.

28

Mardee now walked to school every morning and to work every noon with purposeful steps. She performed her usual tasks with excellence and spoke few unnecessary words to anyone. Raquel was the only person besides Mrs. Roberts in whom she confided. Both gave her unconditional loyalty and understanding.

At work, John was curious when he read the announcement of the coming wedding of Heather and Jeff, but he didn't ask any questions. He knew Jeff had been instrumental in getting Mardee her job, and he had seen the electricity between the two when they were together. He was surprised when it turned out Jeff was going to marry someone else. Inwardly, he felt pleased. Perhaps now Mardee would pay more attention to him.

Thanksgiving week was beautiful; the recent storm was over and the snow was melting in the golden sunny days of Indian Summer. Mardee looked forward to a break, and some of her optimism reasserted itself as she thought about Thanksgiving in the country.

Raquel's parents' ranch near La Cienega was about ten miles southwest of Santa Fe. The large adobe home, built almost one hundred years ago, nestled in a grove of cedar and pinon trees. Miguel Sanchez ran a large herd of cattle in the wooded foothills on the many acres of land that had been given to his ancestors from the King of Spain when they came to settle the new country. The original Spanish cattle had been replaced by sturdy Herefords from Texas that wintered well in the high altitude.

Miguel Sanchez had been educated in Saint Louis, and after marrying Teresa Munez from a neighboring ranch, settled down to run the ranch in a businesslike manner. Raquel was their only child, and she was the star of their lives.

When Raquel had asked her parents for permission to invite Mardee to their home for Thanksgiving, they readily agreed. But when Raquel wanted to include Stewart and Frankie, that was an issue to ponder. They hesitated to agree with this plan.

"Frankie is a special friend of Mardee's," Raquel cajoled. "He is far from home on a holiday. If we don't invite him he will have no one to celebrate with. And Stewart is a soldier in the army of his country. Mama, he would love your good cooking."

Finally, the parents gave in.

"Very well," Miguel Sanchez said in resignation. "We will go into early Mass at the Saint Francis Cathedral on Thanksgiving morning. We will then pick up our guests and bring them home to the ranch for dinner. Does that please you, querida, no?"

"Oh yes," Raquel said, delighted. "You can show them your ranch, Papa. They will be interested in your cows and your horses and your alfalfa fields."

"Machacha, I know what they will be interested in," Mr. Sanchez said as he tweaked Raquel's shiny black curls. "But you are right that we should share with these two people far from their homes. We will be happy to help them have a happy Thanksgiving."

Mardee had then passed the invitations to Stewart and Frankie. "I hope you can eat hot chili," she teasingly told Stewart.

"I'll try," he said, his pink face turning red.

"And don't you look too much at Raquel, Frankie," Mardee warned with a smile. "You are being invited because of me, you know."

"Don't worry," Frankie replied. He was looking forward to seeing Mardee one more time before he had to leave for Belen to go back to work.

The old spark in her eyes is coming back, Frankie thought. He had seen the wedding announcement in the paper at his hotel and was pleased that a very big obstacle had been removed from his ultimate objective. She will be mine, he promised himself.

On Thanksgiving Day Mrs. Sanchez stayed home to prepare dinner, and Miguel and Raquel picked up their guests as planned.

"How was church?" Mardee asked.

"It is a special blessing to go to Mass at Saint Francis Cathedral," Miguel answered. "It is a very beautiful building."

"I must visit that church," Mardee said excitedly. "Frankie, would you come with me?"

"I will try," he said. "I would like to see Bishop Lamy's church before I leave."

Mardee didn't like hearing about Frankie's leaving, but before she could say anything, Mr. Sanchez said, "We usually go to our San Jose Church in La Cienega, but a few times a year we come to Saint Francis on special days."

The conversation then turned to cattle and horses, and Mardee, losing interest, stared out the car windows at the countryside. There was little snow left from last week's storm, and the air was still and crystal clear under an intensely blue sky. The cedars and pinons were lush dark green from the moisture, and the horizon seemed to stretch forever. What a land, this New Mexico, Mardee thought as she relaxed against the back seat. And how wonderful to be out in the country again!

Teresa Sanchez greeted everyone warmly as they drove up to the haciendo. Inside, the warm house was alive with tantalizing smells. Thick logs crossed the low ceilings, and a mud-brick corner fireplace crackled a bright welcome. A long table laden with steaming food dominated one end of the living room.

Miguel took their coats as Teresa ushered them to the festive table. They all stood behind their heavy Spanish style chairs until Miguel rejoined them, and then they all sat. There was traditional turkey, potatoes and gravy, along with corn, baked squash, and pinto beans. A bowl of spicy red chili dominated the middle of the table, adding a bright splash of color. Small goblets of a richly purple drink were placed at each plate.

Everyone waited while Miguel bowed his head and said grace and crossed himself and then raised his head. "Welcome to our table. Enjoy our food." Then he raised his goblet. "First, we will drink a toast."

Everyone raised their goblets as directed. Mardee looked at the intriguing drink, wondering what it was.

Miguel raised his glass higher. "To God with our thanks for all our blessings, to our guests with a prayer for their well being, and to our beautiful state of New Mexico for its new statehood. Everyone drink!"

"To the good winemaker," Frankie said as he raised his glass for a second toast.

"To Mama," Miguel said, "and to Raquel who picked the choke-cherries."

After the toasts as the dishes were passed around, Mardee watched when Stewart took a generous spoonful of red chili and spread it over his potatoes like the others were doing. She caught his eye and shook her head slightly as he started to take another spoonful. He smiled and put the spoon back and passed the chili on.

After everyone had been served Mardee kept her eyes on Stewart when he took a big bite of the potatoes and chili. His face instantly turned a dark red, and an audible gasp escaped his throat. He grabbed for his wine to put out the fire in his mouth.

All eyes turned toward him as he struggled to catch his breath. Teresa quickly ran to the kitchen pump for a large glass of water. "Drink," she commanded. "And take some bites of your tortilla."

Stewart finally got enough of his voice back to whisper, "I'm sorry. It's kind of hot."

Everyone burst into laughter. "Take small bites, Stewart," Mardee directed. "That chili is too hot for an Illinois boy."

"It's very spicey," Stewart said looking over at Mrs. Sanchez. "But it's very good."

After a dessert of apples baked in cinnamon and butter topped with whipped cream, as well as pumpkin pie topped with whipped cream, the diners pushed their chairs back, and the women started to clean the table.

"Come with me," Miguel directed Frankie and Stewart. "I will show you the horses and the cattle."

As the men left Raquel turned to her mother. "You have worked all morning. Now it is your turn to rest. Mardee and I will clean up the kitchen, and then we will take a walk."

The girls worked quickly and soon had a sparkling kitchen. "Let's go," Raquel said, as they headed out the door to join the men. They found them at the corrals admiring Miguel's horses.

"Do you want to ride?" Raquel asked. Mardee nodded her head excitedly. "Papa, help us saddle up the horses. Mardee and I want to go for a ride. Do you want to join us?" she asked, turning to Frankie and Stewart.

Both sets of eyes lit up at the invitation. "Of course, I would love to try out one of these good horses," Stewart answered.

"I would welcome a ride," Frankie added.

Soon the horses were saddled and ready to go. Miguel looked at the sun. "Be back in two hours," he directed, "so I can get you back to town before it's too late."

The two couples rode off with light hearts and quickly decided to go in separate directions. Mardee and Frankie soon came to a little draw where water ran over the red sandstone when it rained. "Let's stop and enjoy the scenery a while," he suggested.

They tied their horses to a scrub cedar tree and sat down on a flat section of rock warmed by the sun.

"This is wonderful," Mardee said, looking around. "Oh, there is a gourd patch. This is just like home," she exclaimed as she grabbed one of the greenish yellow balls and threw it at Frankie.

Frankie tossed it aside and didn't reply for a few moments. "Mardee, I want to talk to you," he said seriously. "This is probably the last chance I'll have, because I'm going back to Belen on Friday."

"I was wondering about that," Mardee said.

"Yes," Frankie said hastily. "I'm needed back in Belen."

The dreaded case, Mardee thought to herself. "Frankie, what is it you're working on? I've heard both you and Papa speak about some case, but I don't know what it is about."

"I can't give you too many details," Frankie said slowly. "I'll just say that there is a gang of men who is robbing the train as it goes over the Manzano Mountains to Mountainair. When the train gets to Amarillo to leave the cars, some of them are empty. The railroad detectives have figured out that the cars are being looted as the train labors slowly over the mountains. It seems the doors have been purposely left unlocked in the Belen Yards, and they just throw out the articles they want. They then carry the stolen goods to a wagon near Scholle and transport it to Albuquerque or Socorro where it is sold.

"This has been going on for some time, but it took a while for the detectives to pinpoint where the crime is being committed. That is why your father was made a special detective so he could investigate in the mountain area. He has done an excellent job of passing along information he has picked up from his mill workers and the others in the area."

"It sounds to me like there is danger involved in trying to catch these men," Mardee said tightly.

"Of course, there is," Frankie answered. "That's why I am going back. They are going to need all the men they can get to catch this gang."

Mardee moved close to Frankie's broad chest. Looking up into his face she said, "I don't want you there, Frankie. I want you here with me."

Frankie quickly put his arm around Mardee's waist and pulled her to him. "I want to be with you, too, Mardee, but I have to go do my job," he said, holding her eyes steadily.

"But what if you or Papa are hurt?" Mardee said as her voice broke.

"There will be several of us there," Frankie reassured her. "But there is always a chance that someone can get hurt. We mean to capture that gang, dead or alive," he added firmly.

Mardee closed her eyes as she felt the warm strongness of Frankie's chest. She had longed for this comforting feeling the last few days. Tears that she had held back so determinedly now pushed against her eyelashes. "Frankie, you always said if I needed you just to call on you. I need you now Frankie, I need you very badly. Don't leave me."

"I know, querida," Frankie said gently. "I know why you need me. I tried to warn you what would happen. But you have a strong head. Tu tienes un cabeza impetuosa. You pay for that, mi hita, in many ways." Frankie looked down at her sadly and then added with a smile, "But you have not only a strong head, you are strong all over. You will get through this time without me, querida. Just think about me, and I will be there in your heart helping you. I have always been with you in my heart ever since you are a little girl. I'm still there, and I will always be there, because I love you, Mardita."

Mardee looked into his dark eyes, suddenly realizing that the love she had always felt for him was stronger than she had realized. "I know, Frankie. I know . . . now." She then returned his kiss from the dormant passion that was just now being kindled. He had kissed her before, but she had never completely returned his passion. Her body answered his probing lips with a demanding challenge filled with fire. She wanted his lips, his kisses, and she wanted his body with an intense desire of overwhelming love.

Frankie suddenly pushed her back and said shakily, "Mardee, what are you doing?"

"I want you," she said huskily. "I love you, and I want only you. I've been so wrong."

Frankie's heart skipped at these words. "Mardee, are you sure you aren't still thinking of Jeff?"

"I'm thinking only of you," Mardee said angrily, "and I don't want you to leave me."

Frankie looked deeply into her teary eyes. "Mardita, listen to me. I have to go. Someday, when the time is right, we will be together. I have things I must do first."

Tapping her trembling lips gently, he added, "Remember what I said, canta y no llores. Always sing, mi hita, and don't cry."

Frankie then helped her up and as he looked into her sad little girl face, he said, "One more kiss, querida, one more kiss. Remember, I have always loved you, and I always will." This is such a sad kiss, Mardee thought. A kiss of goodbye. And she felt her body turn cold.

As they rode back toward the hacienda they met Raquel and Stewart coming from the other direction. The girls then went to the house as the men unsaddled the horses and put them in the corral. They poured themselves glasses of cool milk and got some pastelitos and hurried to Raquel's bedroom to enjoy their refreshments.

Raquel didn't notice Mardee's silence as she excitedly told of her outing with Stewart. "He's so nice and so bashful!" she said, laughing. "He turns red so often . . . what you call it . . . blushes so much!" she announced with a merry laugh.

Mardee suddenly felt weary and old as she listened to her friend's girlish chatter. It seemed like years since she had been in that stage of a romance. She doesn't know how sad and hurtful love can be, she thought darkly as she waved to Frankie from the upstairs window.

Miguel soon took the men back to town, and Mardee stayed with Raquel. She would be with the Sanchez family the whole Thanksgiving vacation.

It was good to be with these warm hospitable people while the sad girl struggled with her heartaches. Teresa Sanchez fussed over her and fed her tasty food, and Miguel smiled his encouragement.

She told Raquel about her new feelings for Frankie, but she didn't tell her of the shadowy premonitions that dominated her thoughts.

Maybe it's just too soon, she thought, to be over the hurt of a broken romance. But she now knew she was falling in love with Frankie. Why do I have the feeling that it is too late? she worried darkly.

29

Mardee went back to school after the Thanksgiving holidays feeling more at peace with her world. The visit with the Sanchezes had been good for her, and now she was looking forward to Christmas when she would return to her beloved home in the Manzano Mountains.

As she hurried down the hall Sister Evangelina motioned to her from her office. She smiled and said, "I want to talk to you for just a few minutes. Sit down. I won't keep you long. I know you have to eat lunch and get to work."

The scared young girl who had once sat in silent awe in this nun's presence now felt a warm confident expectation. She had come to love all the nuns in this school, and she knew they had helped her develop in more ways than just scholastically.

Sister Evangelina smiled again. "It doesn't seem possible, but this semester will be over when we take our Christmas break. You have done exceptionally well; I'm sure your grades will be excellent. I wish all our students were like you."

Mardee smiled. "Thank you so much, Sister," she replied quietly.

"Although I would love to keep you here forever," Sister Evangelina continued, "I think, in all honesty, that we have done all we can do for you. Your high school education is nicely rounded out. It is time for you to think of going to a school of higher education like Saint John's College or the College of Santa Fe. You might even want to go to Albuquerque to the University of New Mexico which is just getting established. Have you thought of going on to college, Mardee?"

"Not really," Mardee said. "I guess I just thought I would be here forever." She felt close to tears at the idea of leaving the Academy. "I'm sorry; I guess I should have been thinking about this."

"It's no problem," Sister Evangelina hastily reassured her. "As I said, we would love to have you here with us forever, but the time has come to think about what is next for you. I will write your father today giving him my thoughts on this matter. And it is something that you can begin to think about seriously. Have you thought about what you would like to do with your life?"

"Not really," Mardee replied softly.

"Well, it's time to start thinking seriously about your future," Sister Evangelina said firmly. "You have the natural talent to become a teacher. You would probably attend the College of Santa Fe for that. You are very talented in singing and drama. If you stay in Santa Fe I would suggest that you become involved with a theater group. We have some people here now who offer workshops in theatrical training. I think you would love getting into the creative arts. So with all your abilities and talents, you see, you do have some choices to think about."

Mardee's mind went almost numb with these new ideas the sister was thrusting upon her. All she'd been thinking about the last few days was going home. "I will consider what you have said, Sister," she said slowly. "Thank you for being concerned for me and advising me. I will talk to my father about your ideas when I go home." Mardee got up slowly and started to leave. "But I can still come back and see you and all the others even if I'm in another school, can't I, Sister?"

"Of course you can, dear. We would be most unhappy if you didn't come back to see us." She then walked her to the door. "Think about what you want to do. I know you're going to make us all proud."

Mardee quickly made her way to the plaza, sat down on a bench, and took her sandwich and apple out of her lunch bag. The sun was shining brightly, and the crisp air felt good. She would sit here a while and maybe she could clear her thoughts. What a fool I am these days, she thought. Of course, I can't stay in the Academy forever.

A pleasant voice suddenly interrupted her thoughts. "Lunch break?" Mardee looked up to find Jeff staring down at her.

"Hello, Jeff," she said tonelessly. Be still my heart, she cautioned herself.

"Could I talk to you a little while?" he asked, sitting down beside her.

"Not another talk," Mardee said with a sigh. "I don't know if I can take too many more of these talks today."

"Who's been talking to you?" Jeff asked curiously.

"Sister Evangelina," Mardee said. "Suddenly I'm faced with decisions that I don't know how to make."

"Career decisions?" Jeff asked knowingly.

"Yes," Mardee replied. "How did you know?"

"It's simple," Jeff said with a smile. "You are obviously not a little high school girl anymore."

"And what do you suggest?" Mardee asked impatiently. "Everyone seems to know more than I about what I should do."

"I think you should be a lawyer," Jeff answered with a teasing smile. "I am very impressed with the work you have done on our education project."

"You know women can't be lawyers," Mardee said with an exasperated shrug.

"Women will be lawyers someday," Jeff said. "It will take someone like Mardee Spencer to make it happen." Jeff paused. "In fact, you can get some experience soon. I have accepted a job in Washington in the legal department there, and Heather and I have changed the date of our marriage. She will be home for Christmas, and we will be married on New Year's Eve. We will leave for the East on New Year's Day, and I will start my new job as soon as I get there."

Mardee felt overwhelmed with this news. Jeff married and gone sooner than expected. What was going to happen next? "That's nice," she muttered.

"Thank you, Mardee. I appreciate your good wishes," Jeff said seriously.

"I am proud of your success in getting such an impressive job," Mardee said sincerely.

"Anyway, Mardee, as I was saying, you can get some legal experience now that I'm leaving for Washington. I have written up the legislation that the governor wants for education. But before it goes to the Legislature in January, I want you to look it over and see if it needs any changes or additions based on the information you get from the sources you are in contact with. If you receive something from another state that you think should go into our education laws, bring it to the governor's attention. He has a great deal of confidence in your good judgment and keen perception."

"Do you think so?" Mardee asked uncertainly.

"I know so," Jeff said. "I'm not the only person who realizes what an outstanding person you are." Jeff then stood up and looked down into the confused eyes of this girl who would always be special to him. "Thank you for your good wishes. It means a great deal to me, Mardee, to know you are still my friend," he said as he hurried away.

"I'm not your friend." Mardee said out loud when he was out of earshot. "I was almost your lover, but I am not your friend."

Mardee sat for a moment in thought. You didn't cry. Good girl! she congratulated herself. I'm all through crying over you, Jeff. I'm dreaming of home and Frankie now, she added with determination.

30

Mardee leaned back against the cushioned seat and closed her eyes. The train swayed in easy rhythm as the wheels clicked along the steel track. "Going home, going home," was the song they sang to the tired girl.

The last weeks before the end of the semester had been busy. There were final reports and tests, as well as preparations for the annual Christmas program. Mardee had played the part of the angel who appeared to Mary telling her she would be the mother of Jesus. The choir had sung Christmas hymns at appropriate times as the story unfolded. Then all the shepherds and angels and wise men had gathered around the manger in tribute to the Baby Jesus as Mardee sang the song, *Away in a Manger.*

When she sang the simple words, Mardee felt her faith soaring, especially while singing the last verse, "Be near me, Lord Jesus, I ask thee to stay, close by me forever, and love me, I pray." Mardee repeated the words to herself now as the shiny train sped down the mountains taking her home.

Mardee had also worked hard on Christmas presents for the Gonzales girls. They would be going to school after Christmas and would need school clothes. Each girl now had two new long skirts and two buttoned blouses for their school adventure. Baby Esperanza also had a pretty bib embroidered with flowers to dress her up for Christmas. Such a doll! Mardee thought.

The mercantile had been a wonderful place to shop for Christmas presents. Mardee had bought knives for her brothers and for Jorje, pretty scarves for Mother Spencer and Mrs. Roberts, and two large tins of Prince Albert smoking tobacco for her father and Judge Roberts. And she had a special present for Frankie carefully packed away in her suitcase amid layers of tissue paper.

Among the figurines at the store she had found a beautiful little hummingbird with a rose red head, green wings, and a creamy white underbody. Just the way Grammy used to describe hummingbirds! she told herself. I'll give this to Frankie as a symbol that I am his hummingbird now. I don't have to fly around looking for honey anymore.

Mardee had drifted off to sleep, but the jolt of the train suddenly brought her back to consciousness. She quickly looked out the window and saw the sign, HARVEY HOUSE. Just then the conductor in his dark uniform came through the car announcing, "Albuquerque, ladies and gentlemen. We are now in Albuquerque, New Mexico." Mardee collected her belongings, her jacket, purse, and the small suitcase.

Indian women were sitting on the platform selling their handmade turquoise jewelry as Mardee got off to change trains. She had nearly two hours to wait, so she decided to look at their wares. I don't have a present for Lola, she thought. She would love a piece of jewelry. A small bracelet caught her eye. It had a green turquoise stone set in a narrow silver band. Lola would like that, she thought, and after a few minutes of haggling she bought the bracelet for one dollar.

She still had nearly an hour before her next train, so she sat down on one of the hard seats in the waiting room. Just as she reached in her suitcase for the book she was reading, *Anna and the King of Siam*, a nicely dressed young man sat down beside her. "Is that an interesting book?" he asked.

"Oh yes," Mardee replied. "It's about an English teacher who goes to Siam to teach the ruler's children. He has many wives, so he has over fifty children."

"I'm Carter McMahan," he said. "I'm a student at the university, and I'm going home for the holidays."

"Where is home?" Mardee asked with interest.

"In Las Cruces," Carter answered.

Las Cruces sounded a million miles away to Mardee. "Oh," she said. "I'm going home for the holidays, also. I'm going to Mountainair, and my father will meet me and take me to our home in the Manzano Mountains.

Eastview is the name of our little town. I don't suppose you've heard of it." Mardee gave the young man an amused smile.

"No, I haven't," Carter answered easily. "But I'm sure it is a wonderful place if it has girls like you there."

"You should come there sometime and see for yourself," Mardee returned just as easily.

Soon the train arrived and both Mardee and Carter boarded. Carter would take this train all the way to Las Cruces, while Mardee would change in Belen. They settled into a seat together, and the time passed quickly for both of them as they chatted like old friends. They pulled into Belen before they knew it.

All thoughts of Carter McMahan were wiped away, however, when Mardee boarded the train for Mountainair. The hour's ride across the flatlands and up the steep mountains seemed like an eternity. Pine trees gave way to cedars and pinons, and as rocky red bluffs passed by the window Mardee knew she was almost home. I'm here, she thought. I'm close to home again!

Mardee spotted her father immediately as she came down the steps of the train. She rushed to him and was about to embrace him when she noticed that his left arm was held in a sling. "Oh Papa!" she said with concern. "What has happened to your arm?"

Ben Spencer put his right arm around Mardee's shoulders and smiled down at her. "Welcome home, Mardeebird. We're so happy to see you. Here are Sadie and Roy." Ben stepped back as Roy rushed forward almost knocking Mardee over with his exuberant hug. Mardee held her little brother tight, realizing how much she had missed him.

Sadie was standing erect with a look of concern on her face. "Hello, Mother Spencer," Mardee said warmly. "It's so good to be home."

"It's good to have you," Sadie said as she stepped forward. "We have missed you." She gave Mardee a stiff hug.

Ben took Mardee's small suitcase. "Is this all your luggage?" he asked.

"I didn't bring too much because I suppose I'll be going back before too long. Did you get a letter from Sister Evangelina?"

"Yes," Ben said as he took Mardee's arm. "We'll discuss that later. Let's get to the car."

Ben opened the back door for Mardee and Sadie. "You can ride in the front with me, son," he said to Roy.

After everyone was settled Ben cranked the car and eased into the driver's seat. He turned the car west and headed up the main street.

"I'll help you with the extra work and holiday baking," Mardee said as she turned to Sadie. "With both Lola and I there, you won't have to do anything." She beamed at her stoic stepmother.

"I'll have to do plenty," Sadie replied dryly. "The school is out for vacation, of course, but I have the Christmas mail rush at the post office as well as yearly government reports to work on. But I will appreciate your help at the house."

"Now what is wrong with your arm, Papa?" Mardee asked again.

Ben slowed down for a dog and negotiated a sharp turn off the main street road before he answered. "It's not serious, Mardee. There's been a little excitement around here lately. I almost got in the way of a bullet, but it only grazed my arm."

"A bullet!" Mardee gasped. "What happened, Papa?"

"We'll talk about it later, Mardee," Ben said firmly. "Anyway, I know you would like to have Sadie tell you what's been happening in the family."

"Well," Sadie said slowly, "Roy has been doing very well in school. He is making all A's, and he has learned the Gettysburg Address. He recited it for the school program. President Lincoln would have been proud of him." Roy put his head down shyly when Mardee reached over the seat to pat his shoulder.

"So you're getting better at standing up in front of people," Mardee said with a smile.

Sadie then went on with what had been happening the past months. She's talking more than usual, Mardee thought as she listened none too closely. "Excuse me, Mother Spencer," she broke in, "but there is no scene so beautiful in the world as the view of the mountains from here. They are spectacular!" Mardee sighed ecstatically, and Sadie glanced at her impatiently.

"Ah, yes," Sadie said, "but I must tell you about the Tompkins family. Old Lou's latest young wife rebelled and took the whip away from him in the field when they were harvesting beans last fall, and then she used it on him. Now she is the boss of the farm, and poor old Lou is too ashamed to come and see us anymore. Lola is very happy she is staying with us because she is afraid of her stepmother."

That's good enough for that horrible old man, Mardee thought. He will get paid back for all his harsh treatment of his wives and children.

Roy suddenly turned in his seat. "John and I got to stay in Old Lou's house while he and his wife went to Isleta to visit. We stayed there all by ourselves, and we weren't afraid. We fed the animals and guarded the house."

"You were brave to do that," Mardee said with enthusiasm.

"And he let us sleep in his big soft bed. It was a nice bed, but there was only one problem." Roy shook his head.

"What was that?" Mardee asked, interested.

"Ugh, you tell her Papa," Roy said shaking his head.

Ben smiled. "The boys couldn't wait to sleep in Old Lou's big feather bed, so they crawled in early the first night and snuggled down under the covers. They had never slept in a bed so fancy. They were enjoying their comfortable bed and about to go to sleep when they started feeling things crawling on them. John got up and lit a lamp and turned back the covers. The bed was alive with reddish brown bugs crawling over the pillows and the quilts."

"They were bedbugs," Roy broke in. "Millions of bedbugs. We never knew so many bedbugs existed."

"Oh dear," Mardee remarked. "So what did you do?"

"We slept on the floor," Roy said. "We never touched that bed again except to pull the covers back up and make the bed look nice for when Old Lou came home. We slept on that floor for three nights."

"So what did you tell Old Lou when he came home?" Mardee asked, trying to contain her laughter.

"We told him it was a good bed, but we didn't tell him we slept in it," Roy said. "He told us getting to sleep in his big bed was our pay for taking care of his place. Not much pay," Roy finished sadly.

"No wonder Old Lou is so ornery," Mardee said. "Sleeping with bedbugs all the time would make anyone mean!"

Sadie broke into the conversation and talked about her students. And Mardee told her about teaching the Gonzales children, the Academy, and all the teachers. She could tell that Sadie genuinely enjoyed hearing about the school.

The school conversation lasted until Ben turned down the lane to the ranch house. Mardee glimpsed Gypsy standing in the pasture. She's all wooly for winter, she thought. She looks like a little burro.

Ben soon brought the car to a stop and they unloaded. Lola was stirring gravy at the stove as they came in. She quickly laid her spoon down and ran to meet Mardee. "Welcome home!" she said earnestly. "You look so pretty. It is wonderful to see you."

Mardee gave Lola a warm hug. "You are the one who looks so pretty. Mother Spencer, are you keeping all the young boys chased away from here?" Lola was maturing into a very attractive young woman.

"Oh yes," Sadie replied. "Lola is too busy with her chores to have time for young men."

Mardee winked at Lola. "The food smells so good," Mardee said taking off her jacket. "Let me help you set the table."

Just then the three older boys came in from their chores, each carrying a pail of milk. "We like to never got Old Red from the pasture to the barn," Floyd announced impatiently. "She's such a stubborn old thing. The other cows always come fine."

"Come over and say hello to your sister," Ben directed quietly. "Then wash up for supper."

"Floyd, you are so tall," Mardee squealed. "And Charlie, you are growing up, too. Have you been practicing your running? You know, we expect you to win in the national race next year. And John, you're taller than I am. I can't believe how much you all have grown!"

The family soon sat down to pot roast, carrots, potatoes, and gravy, which tasted as good as Mardee had remembered. When it came time for dessert, Mother Spencer went into the pantry and brought out a pie topped with hills of fluffy meringue. "Lemon pie," she announced. "Lemon pie to celebrate Mardee's homecoming."

"Oh, Mother Spencer," Mardee exclaimed. "Thank you so much."

"You are welcome," Sadie said with a smile. "I hope it is good."

When supper was over Ben turned to Mardee. "Come in the living room with me, Mardee," he said in a serious tone. "Sadie and Lola will clean up the kitchen."

She pushed back her chair, thanked Sadie and Lola for the meal, and followed her father. Ben and Mardee sat down on the divan which had a new flowered cover, Mardee noticed.

"We have something to talk about," he said. "Mardee, I told you we had some excitement around here a few nights ago. There was gunfire exchanged, and I was wounded, as I told you."

"Who exchanged the gunfire, Papa?" Mardee asked, her whole body paralyzed with dread.

"A gang of train robbers and a posse of lawmen," Ben answered.

"The gang that has been robbing the train as it came over the mountains?" Mardee whispered.

"Yes," Ben replied.

"And . . . and Frankie?"

"Frankie was shot also," Ben said. "He was more seriously hurt than I was."

"Oh no, Papa," Mardee said frantically. "He's not dead, Papa. Tell me he's not dead."

Ben put his arms around his daughter. "He was shot in the chest. He died." Ben said quietly.

Mardee crumpled in her father's arms. "Not Frankie, not Frankie."

"Yes, Mardee," her father said. "He died in the hospital in Albuquerque yesterday."

Mardee collapsed on the divan as Sadie rushed to her side. "Let's get her upstairs, Spencer. I'll sit with her."

Ben and Sadie slowly helped Mardee up the stairs, and Sadie gently undressed her and took her warm nightgown from her suitcase. "Don't break Frankie's Christmas present," the distraught young woman whispered hoarsely.

"I won't," Sadie said calmly as she gently closed the suitcase. She then pulled the nightgown carefully over Mardee's head and down over her shaking body and covered her gently with blankets.

"You must rest, dear. I'll sit here by your bed in case you need anything."

"I need Frankie," Mardee said between sobs. "I didn't know I'd always loved him until too late. I was going to tell him. Now it's too late," she sobbed.

Sadie quickly went to get a cold wet cloth and washed Mardee's hot tearstained face. "It's all right, Mardee. God will help you," she kept repeating. "You know the Bible says that God never gives us more to bear than our shoulders can carry. Ask God to help you, Mardee."

Mardee sat up fighting mad at these words. "I'm getting tired of carrying all the burdens God thinks I'm strong enough to carry. I don't want to hear about the Bible, Mother Spencer, and I don't want to hear about God."

Sadie shook her head sadly and closed her eyes in prayer.

Mardee fell back onto the bed breathing heavily. The silence hung in the air, both women in their own worlds.

"Who were the train robbers?" Mardee finally asked. "How were they caught?"

"It was a family from Scholle," Sadie explained with relief in her voice. "It was a father and two sons and a son-in-law. There was a brother-in-law who lives in Belen and works for the railroad in the yards there who was helping them. He would leave certain cars unlocked that were to be put on trains going east. Then he would get word to the other gang members. They would lie in wait and board the train as it moved slowly through the mountains and throw the merchandise off. They would then take the stolen cargo to Belen or Socorro or Albuquerque and sell it to merchants who asked no questions.

"This has been going on for about a year now. When the railroad detectives finally determined that the crimes were being committed in the Manzano Mountains, your father was appointed as a special deputy."

"And he found out what was happening?" Mardee asked dully.

"Yes," Sadie replied. "The two sons work here at the mill. They aren't too smart, and your father was suspicious about a few things they said. They were getting overly confident since they had been getting away with the robberies so long."

"That's when Frankie was called back?" Mardee asked.

"Yes," Sadie said. "Frankie stayed here most of the time since he returned. He would ride out at night and check the railroad. He finally pinpointed the place where the men were climbing on the train. He could tell by the horse tracks and small pieces of things that had broken as they had been tossed off the train. He followed the tracks through the trees until he found the wagon stashed in some undergrowth. He then followed the trail the wagon took into the valley where things were sold. One of the railroad detectives in Belen had seen one of the gang fooling with the locks on the cars. That man was arrested and persuaded to talk. He turned state's evidence so he could save his own neck. He told the detectives who his partners were and when they would rob the next train. A posse hid out and waited. The gang was captured, but your father was wounded, and Frankie was shot in the chest. That's the story, dear." Sadie paused and added, "Remember the man the deputy from Belen came here looking for?"

Mardee silently nodded her head.

"He was one of the gang members," Sadie concluded.

Mardee was now in control of her feelings. "I think I have known what was going to happen," she said finally. "I have had a premonition about this case ever since Papa first mentioned it."

"That does happen sometimes," Sadie said. "God was probably trying to prepare you. One thing you should know, Mardee, is that your father and Frankie became very close while they worked together on this case. Your father grew to respect Frankie very much. He is also grieving over this tragedy."

"This must have been so hard for you, Mother Spencer," she said with compassion. "Thank God Papa wasn't badly hurt."

"I have said many prayers for your father in the last few months," Sadie said simply. "I guess I should have said more for Frankie."

"No, I should have done that, and I didn't," Mardee said flatly. "God forgive me for being so thoughtless."

Just then Ben Spencer appeared in the doorway. "How are you doing, Mardeegirl?"

"I'm all right, Papa," Mardee said weakly. "I'm so thankful that you are all right," she added as tears brimmed over.

"That's the way it goes, darlin'," Ben said with a slight twinkle in his eyes. "God takes the good to help him. He leaves the bad here to struggle on."

"Oh Papa," Mardee said as the tears rushed out again.

Ben sat on the side of her bed and softly patted her hand. "There, there, Mardeebird. We're with you. You'll be all right."

Sadie left to get another cool washcloth.

"When is the funeral?" Mardee asked finally.

"It's in two days," Ben answered. "On Christmas Eve in the church at Punta."

31

For Mardee, the next few days were a cloudy haze of dim faces and sketchy words. But there were supportive arms and compassionate tears as she wrestled with the reality of this tragedy.

She vaguely remembered standing beside Frankie's casket in the church and seeing him lying as if asleep, but when she kissed his mouth she was shocked by the cold hardness of those pale lips. Her father had caught her swaying body and helped her back to the very bench on which she and Frankie had sat at his mother's funeral only a few months ago. She would always remember certain words the Santa Fe Railroad official had spoken in his tribute to Frank Moseby: courageous, diligent, smart, and brave. There were similar words from her father: loyal, dependable, ambitious, fearless. Yes, he's fearless, she thought bitterly. He's all those things, but he's dead.

Mardee remembered walking numbly behind the casket as it was carried from the church, her father holding her arm on one side and Frankie's father on the other side. As they stood by the graveside someone said to her, "You can always be proud of the way he died."

"I'm proud of the life he lived," Mardee had replied.

As Mardee watched the casket lowered into the ground, all emotion had drained from her body. He's not there, she said fiercely to herself. He's not trapped in that box in the ground. He's in heaven with God and his mother. Her shattered heart splintered even more as she glanced at the ashen face of Mr. Moseby. The words "so alone, so alone," pulsated through her senses. Dear God, so alone.

The funeral was on Christmas Eve. That evening the family celebrated its usual traditions. Sadie read the Christmas story, and Ben led everyone in singing Christmas carols. Mardee shut her eyes tightly and clenched her hands as the last verse of *Away in a Manger* was sung. She listened intently: "Be near me, Lord Jesus, I ask thee to stay, close by me forever, and love me, I pray; bless all the dear children in thy tender care, and take us to heaven to live with thee there." This would always be the prayer for Frankie and her.

After the singing everyone was allowed to open one present. The boys whooped with pleasure over their new knives from Mardee, and Lola's eyes were round with awe at the Indian bracelet. She had never had jewelry before. Ben smiled his pleasure over the tin of Prince Albert, and Sadie tied her silk scarf around her neck in a prim bow.

"Wonderful presents," Ben said. "It's a thrill to get things from Santa Fe, Mardee."

Then Ben left the room and returned with a prettily wrapped box. "Frankie left this for you in case he couldn't be here on Christmas Day," he said quietly.

Mardee gently accepted the small box, her heart pounding. She carefully removed the ribbon and paper and slowly opened the box. A gold locket in the shape of a heart lay inside. "It's so beautiful," she said softly.

"Look inside," Roy said.

The opened locket revealed a small picture of Frankie. His serious dark eyes contrasted with the mischievous grin on his face. "What does it say there?" Roy asked, looking over her shoulder.

Mardee peered closely at the inside rim. A few words were inscribed in a delicate scroll. "I love you," she read tremulously.

"Did Frankie love you?" Roy said with big eyes.

"Yes," Mardee said slowly. "He said he had loved me always, and that he always would love me."

"Do you love him?" Roy asked curiously.

"I'm sure I do," Mardee replied. "I think I have always loved him." She marveled at how calm she felt. "Always tell people you love them before it is too late, Roy."

* * *

Mardee remembered very little about Christmas Day or the days that followed. She stayed mostly in her room with her tears and her grief. She touched the locket around her neck often, thinking each time that Frankie had touched it, too. Just knowing that brought her comfort.

She went through the motions of eating and helping with the chores. "Leave her alone," Ben said wisely to everyone. "She has much grieving to do now. Her strong spirit will reassert itself eventually."

A week into the new year, Mardee suddenly felt the impulse to take her father's lunch to him at the mill as she always had done in the past. When she walked past the crew working on their various tasks, she suddenly felt her interest in life returning. She even waved to some of the men who had worked so long for her father and felt a smile forming on her face. Seeing the old familiar scenes and hearing the whining of the saw brought her a strange comfort. Life goes on, she thought in surprise.

Opening the door to her father's office brought the same old feeling of happy expectation she had always had. "Hello, Papa," she said, almost merrily. "I brought your lunch."

"Good, I'm starved," he said, as usual.

Motioning her to the old leather chair, he continued, "I'm glad you're here. You got a letter today from the governor."

It had been so long since she had thought about the governor and her job, and now it was difficult to discipline her thoughts back to reality. Life in Santa Fe seemed like make-believe now. "Open the letter and read it, dear," Ben said gently.

Mardee swiftly skimmed over the first part in which the governor expressed his sympathy about Frankie and his concern for her father. Then she came to a paragraph that grabbed her attention. "I'm sure you know that Jeff Corbin has accepted a job in Washington," the governor wrote. "He is taking John Weeks with him as an aide. That leaves John's position open, and I would like to offer it to you. In your time with us you have proven yourself to be very efficient and capable, and I feel confident that you can handle this position.

"This is a full-time job, of course, and I do not know what your school plans are, so perhaps this would not work out for you. But I want you to know that you are my first choice for the position, and I would appreciate your letting me know immediately. John will be leaving the fifteenth of January, and I must have someone here by that date."

Mardee looked up at her father with wide eyes. "Papa, the governor wants me to be his aide," she said.

Ben quickly took the letter, and when he had finished reading it he looked over at Mardee with wide eyes. "You are right," he said excitedly. "Mardee, this is almost unbelievable!"

"I can do John's job," Mardee said confidently. "I helped him enough to know what he does. I can do it."

"But we've got to think of school," Ben said thoughtfully. "I tell you what, Mardeegirl, you go home and think about this offer, and we'll talk about it after supper."

Mardee left her father's office with her usual quick steps. Santa Fe was now very much on her mind. She clasped her locket with one hand. "Frankie, it looks like I'm going back to the lights of Santa Fe!"

32

As Mardee approached the house she noticed a strange car coming up the lane. Who could that be? she wondered, staring at the unfamiliar vehicle.

A hand waved out the window. "Hello, Mardee! Remember me?"

The mystery driver got out of his car. "Don't you remember your old traveling partner, Carter McMahan? I thought I made more of an impression on you," he laughingly said.

"Oh," Mardee smiled, recognition dawning on her face. "I'm sorry. Of course, I remember you."

"You invited me to Eastview, so I decided to take you up on your invitation. I'm on my way back to the university, and I thought I'd take a little detour and say hello."

Carter walked over with long steps, pushing back his tousled dark brown hair which fell over laughing brown eyes. A boyish smile lit his face with pleasure. Mardee hadn't noticed how tall he was in their first brief encounter. As he reached out with his long arms and grasped Mardee's hands, she caught her breath and stepped back.

Carter quickly stepped back as well. "I didn't mean to startle you. I am just glad to see you."

He looked down into the beautiful face he couldn't get out of his mind, and he detected a paleness and a brooding sadness in the magnificent turquoise eyes that hadn't been there before. His heart was as large as his big body, and he sensed the pain she was experiencing.

"I'd like to visit with you a little while if it's all right," he said kindly. "My father gave me this car when I was home for Christmas. I'm mighty proud of it. It has literally flown all the way up here. I'd like to take you for a ride." He added with a shy grin, "It's a Model EMF, 30, Studebaker."

Mardee looked up into this rugged face with the kind smile and remembered she had found him pleasant, but he hadn't made much of an impression on her one way or another because all her thoughts had been on Frankie at that time. He looks like a man of strength and perception, she thought, and he's certainly very handsome in an unsophisticated way.

"Let's walk over to the post office and the mill and meet my parents. Then we'll talk about the ride. How did you find me?" she asked as they headed for the post office.

"You told me you live in Eastview," Carter said, smiling. "I just followed the road." He paused for a moment. "Actually, I drove to Mountainair and got directions."

"But why did you really come?" Mardee persisted, looking up with perplexed eyes.

"I wanted to see you, of course," Carter replied. "I was very intrigued with that girl I met in the Albuquerque train station. But what really brought me was what I have been reading in the newspaper."

"The newspaper?" Mardee asked quickly.

"Stories about a gang of train robbers captured here in the mountains. I read about Special Deputy Ben Spencer being wounded. I associated that name with Mardee Spencer."

"Yes, he's my father," Mardee said quietly.

"Is he all right?" Carter asked anxiously.

"Yes," Mardee answered. "He was only grazed in the arm. The wound is healing nicely. It's nice of you to come by and check on him."

They walked on in silence for a few moments, and then Carter said hesitantly, "And the other man who was killed, Frank Moseby."

"Yes?" Mardee asked in a tight voice.

"Was that the Frankie you mentioned?" Carter cast a concerned look at Mardee.

"Yes," Mardee answered. "I got home in time to go to his funeral."

"I'm so sorry," Carter said.

"Thank you," Mardee replied. "I can't really talk about this yet. I hope you understand." Mardee fought back her tears and quickly changed the subject, "That's the post office. My mother works there."

After introductions, Sadie's usual sour expression lightened when Carter remarked that he had never known a woman postmistress before. "Only men postmasters," he said with a grin.

"Mother Spencer can do anything," Mardee explained. "She is also the teacher in our one-room school."

"I am certainly impressed," Carter remarked.

It was not in Sadie's nature to take compliments gracefully. "It's nice to meet you, Mr. McMahan, but I am busy. You two had better be on your way," she said, returning to her familiar disapproving demeanor, but Mardee noticed there was a slight smile playing at the corners of her mouth.

"It's a pleasure, ma'am," Carter said, poking his large hand through the window. "I hope to see you again sometime." He shook Sadie's hand vigorously, and she looked relieved when he turned loose.

"What a nice lady," he commented as they headed for the mill. "But she doesn't look like you," he said in a puzzled tone.

"She's my stepmother," Mardee explained quickly, "but I consider her my real mother."

"That's good," Carter said with a perplexed shake of his head.

"You are surprised that I have a nice stepmother who is also a postmistress," Mardee commented, laughing.

"I guess so," Carter answered with a grin.

As they neared the mill Mardee spotted her father talking to his edgerman. Ben looked up with interested surprise as he turned around to greet his visitors. "Papa, this is Carter McMahan from Las Cruces. Carter, this is my father, Ben Spencer." As the two men shook hands, Mardee added, "I met Carter on the train coming home."

"I read in the paper about the railroad escapade here," Carter remarked. "I stopped by on my way back to school in Albuquerque to see how you are, sir. Mardee tells me you are healing fine. I am so glad to hear that, and I want to congratulate you on your success in capturing that gang."

"I thank you for your concern," Ben replied as his eyes assessed the man addressing him. "We had enough good men, and they didn't have a chance with us. They will be put away a long time for murder, as well as robbery. They thought there was no law up here in these mountains. They found out differently."

As Ben led them down to his office, Carter continued, "My father is Bill McMahan in Las Cruces. He runs a ranch as well as a business in town. He has race horses, and he told me to check with you about the Steeldust breed. He has heard that you own a good running horse."

"Yep," Ben answered, "that's right. My Diablo horse beats everything around here easily. I got him in Texas from the original Steeldust breeders. I've been very happy with my investment."

The men talked race horses, and Mardee walked along with her own thoughts. How interesting that Carter should walk back into my life at this time. He and Papa seem to hit it off very well, she mused.

"I'm sorry, but you're going to have to excuse me," Ben said when they reached his office. "I would like to continue this talk, and we will at a later date, but I must help with the loading of an order that goes out today. Mardee, take Carter over to the barn and show our black devil horse to him," he directed.

The two men shook hands warmly. "Carter wants to take me for a ride in his new car, Papa. Is that all right?"

"It won't be a very long ride," Carter hastened to add. "I've got to be on my way soon."

"That's fine," Ben said hastily. "I'll see you again, Carter." He saluted with a friendly smile and turned back to his work as Mardee led Carter to the horse barn.

"What's wrong?" Mardee asked tenderly as she offered some oats to Diablo. "Hasn't Floyd taken you out for a run lately? He should take better care of our beautiful boy." The horse chewed the oats and blew loudly through his nostrils.

Carter stood back and looked the horse over carefully. "No wonder he can run," he said with awe. "What a gorgeous creature. He's got all the signs of strength and speed." As Mardee fed the horse and patted his forehead, Carter circled him and remarked on his strong racing points. "Long legs, strong withers, wonderful muscle tone. What a beauty! He's smart, too, I can tell by his eyes."

"Oh yes, he's all those things," Mardee said. "But you should see my horse, Gypsy. She will beat him in a short race."

"Is that the little mare I saw in the pasture as I drove up?" Carter asked.

"Yes," Mardee said with great satisfaction.

Carter pushed his hair back from his forehead with his big hand and grinned crookedly, "I kind of doubt that, Mardee. No offense," he added quickly.

"Well, if we're both here next summer I'll show you." Mardee turned a stubborn face up toward Carter's laughing eyes.

"Well," Carter said. "I'm going to tell my dad to invest in some Steeldust horses. I've never seen a horse so spectacular as this one." Taking Mardee's arm, he said, "If we are going to have time for a ride in my new car, we'd better go."

Lola was standing in the doorway as they returned to the car. "Come and join us," Mardee said as she thought, I'll get even with you for that remark about my horse.

Lola excitedly ran out, and as Carter opened the door for her to get in the back seat, he said with a smile that was almost sincere, "I'd rather have two pretty girls than one anytime."

Mardee got in the front seat and looked over at Carter mischievously. He returned her look with a sly wink of an eye. I'll get even with you for this, was the silent message in his eyes.

"This is where I went to school," Mardee said as they approached the rock school. "Lola went there, also. Let's stop and pay a visit."

They walked around the building, peering into windows. "It looks the same," Mardee said. "The same desks and blackboards. The same picture of

Old George up in the front of the room. The same big potbellied stove. We used to put our chairs in a circle around the stove to keep warm. We looked forward to reading class because it was warmer there than at our desks."

"I went to a school similar to this one," Carter said, "but when I got older my mother moved into Las Cruces in the winter time to send me to school in town. But I'm convinced that these were great schools. The older students helped the younger ones, and the older ones had daily review on all their subjects as the younger ones had their classes."

"I may become a teacher," Mardee said. "I love to work with children. I taught some little Spanish children to read in Santa Fe. They hadn't been to school before, but they learned fast, and I've talked their mother into sending them to public school now."

"Good for you," Carter remarked. "What were you doing in Santa Fe?"

"I work for the governor there. Do you know Governor McDonald?"

"No, but I hear good things about him. How amazing to have a job with the governor at your young age."

"I'm not so young," Mardee said quietly. "Not so young any more."

"What do you do?" Carter asked, obviously very interested.

"I am an interpreter and an advisor to the governor. I will be a full-fledged aide when I go back on the fifteenth. I have also worked on some education legislation for him. I enjoy that kind of work very much. In fact, I am thinking about taking some night courses at the College of Santa Fe when I go back–some pre-law courses."

"Pre-law courses!" Carter exploded. "You are a surprise a minute. Are you serious?"

"Of course, I'm serious," Mardee retorted. "Don't you think I can manage law courses?"

Carter put out a big hand as if to ward off an attack. "I would never think that, believe me. I am convinced that you can do anything you set your mind to. Isn't that right, Lola?" he said, bringing the quiet girl into the conversation.

"Oh yes," Lola said, beaming. "Mardee can learn anything."

"You can, too, Lola," Mardee said, shaking her finger at the younger girl.

Carter looked at the sun. "I'd like to stay here forever, girls," he drawled, "but I've got to get on my way to the big city. Vacation time is over for me." He looked down at the vibrant girl at his side and continued. "Mardee Spencer, I'm glad I met you. I like everything about you, your hair, your eyes, your smart head, and your ambition. But if I'm going to be your biggest supporter, I need to come to Santa Fe to see you occasionally." Carter paused and looked straight down into the greenish-blue eyes turned up to him. "Will it be all right if I come to visit?"

"Not for a while," Mardee answered with a slight tremor in her voice. "But maybe sometime. You can find me in the governor's office."

"I'll remember that," Carter said. Taking one of her little hands, he raised it gently to his lips and brushed it lightly with a kiss. "Thank you for spending time with me. You have made me look forward to my next semester. Remember," he said seriously, "if you want to study law, you do it, and I pray to God I never have to oppose you in a case."

"You're studying to be a lawyer?" Mardee asked. "Well, Carter McMahan, you're full of surprises, too."

As Carter drove off with a flourish, Mardee thought, Thanks Mr. Carter McMahan. I think you have helped me decide what I am going to do with my life!

33

When the girls arrived back at the house, Mardee collapsed in one of the kitchen chairs and said breathlessly, "Oh, I feel so alive. It's so good to feel the cold air on my cheeks."

"It's good to hear you laugh again," Lola said smiling. "You are really back with us now, the same wonderful Mardee."

"Come on, let's get supper going," Mardee said. "How about stew with meat from the roast yesterday. Cut up the meat, and I'll peel some potatoes. Go to the cellar and get small jars of carrots, green beans, and tomatoes. I'll cut up an onion. And bring a large jar of canned peaches for dessert. We haven't had time to cook anything, but they will be delicious with cream. I love Mother Spencer's canned fruit."

Soon the hungry working people came trooping in. Mardee had added a little red chili pepper to the stew. "That will make it taste good on this cold winter day," Mardee told Lola.

Everyone sat down to big bowls of spicy stew, homemade rolls and butter, and large glasses of cold milk.

"Wait, boys," Ben directed as they picked up their spoons. "We will have a prayer." Sadie raised her eyebrows; Ben never said grace. Everyone bowed their heads in wonder, and Ben clasped his hands, bowed his head, and began, "Dear Lord, we thank you for the food set before us. We thank you for all our blessings and especially for the hands that prepared our food. Be with us always, leading, guiding, and directing. In Jesus' name we pray. Amen."

"Thank you, Spencer," Sadie said with a rare smile. "That was nice."

Ben winked at Mardee and took a big bite. "Delicious!" he murmured.

After the girls had cleaned up the kitchen, Mardee went into the living room where her father was reading a magazine.

"Papa, could you come with me. Remember, we need to talk, and I want to visit Grammy's grave."

"Of course," Ben said, putting his magazine down.

"Bring some wire," Mardee asked. "I want to hang a present up for Grammy while there's still light enough."

Ben put his jacket on and reached for a strand of wire hanging from a nail outside. "Yes, we must talk about school and your job offer," he said.

"Papa, I have decided I really want to work for the governor. And I can save some money. Maybe I will want to go to school in Albuquerque eventually."

"Why Albuquerque?" Ben asked with interest.

"I may want to get a law degree," Mardee replied, watching her father's face for his reaction.

Whatever Ben was thinking didn't show on his face. "I can understand that," he said slowly. "I have often wished I had more education. I would like to have been a lawyer myself."

"Really, Papa? You would have been such a good lawyer," Mardee said with enthusiasm.

"Well, it just wasn't meant to be," Ben said. "But you realize that isn't the usual profession for a woman."

"I know, Papa," Mardee said with a sigh. "But it's what I want to do. I could take some pre-law night courses at the Santa Fe College. Then when Governor McDonald is out of office, I could go to the University of New Mexico and really start working for a degree. How does that sound?"

"Your plans sound very good to me. But when did you get interested in law?"

"I guess when Governor McDonald let me work on researching education laws and helping prepare legislation for education in the state. I found it fascinating. There have been some things that happened since, but I think that was when I first became interested in law."

"You worked with Jeff?" Ben asked.

"A little," Mardee said, "but I did most of it myself. Jeff was gone. He was gone on the business of getting himself a wife." Mardee smiled wryly and added, "I really don't care anymore."

At the big yellow pine Ben reached down and picked up a weed that had entangled itself around the faded headboard. "She's been gone four years," he said quietly. "I still miss her."

"I do too, Papa, but I think she is always with me. I know she helps me all the time," Mardee said quietly.

"I'm sure she does," Ben said sadly.

"See, Papa, I want to hang this little hummingbird on a branch over her grave if we can. I was going to give this to Frankie, but now I want it over her grave to remind her that I'm always thinking about her. You know she called me her little hummingbird, Papa."

"Yes, she did," Ben said with a smile.

With Mardee's help Ben put the wire around a small branch and through a small hole in the top of the figurine's wing, and then he twisted the wire together. "How's that?" he asked as he stepped back.

"That looks pretty," Mardee said, looking up at the little bird. Then turning to her father, she said, "You know, Papa, I was just thinking. People like you and me, and Mother Spencer and the boys, and Frankie and Lola, and Jorje and Baby Esperanza in Santa Fe, we are the ones who will build the new state of New Mexico. I love this state, and I understand our people. I know I can play a positive part in helping New Mexico develop. It's exciting to think about playing a role in this great drama!"

"Always wanting to be on the stage," Ben said teasingly.

Mardee's eyes were drawn back to the little hummingbird. It swayed gracefully as the last glint of winter sun reflected off its bright wings. Pointing a finger upward, she said softly, "Look, Papa, I have Grammy's and Frankie's blessings."

"I'm sure," Ben said softly as he looked into his daughter's glowing face framed by the sun's reflection on her red-gold hair.